PAST PERFECT

Gregg was standing on a makeshift stage at the end of the huge room. He waved his hands to quiet everyone and then began his campaign speech. His sincerity came through loud and clear, and it was easy for Laurie to see why he hadn't had any trouble making friends in their new school.

Laurie felt a rush of pride and sadness as she listened. She couldn't hope to hold on to Gregg for herself any longer. He had moved ahead with his new life, and now Laurie would have to do the same—before she lost him for good. The only trouble was, she didn't know where to start.

Bantam Sweet Dreams Romances
Ask your bookseller for the books you have missed

Past Perfect

Fran Michaels

BANTAM BOOKS
TORONTO • NEW YORK • LONDON • SYDNEY • AUCKLAND

RL 6, IL age 11 and up

PAST PERFECT
A Bantam Book/July 1988

ISBN 0-553-26789-2

Published simultaneously in the United States and Canada

Printed and bound in Great Britain by
Cox & Wyman Ltd., Reading

With all my love
to a very special mother—mine

Chapter One

"Liz, will you mail this on your way to the library?" Laurie Raymond pleaded, stepping out onto the patio to hand a lavender envelope to her sister.

"*Oooh*, what is this? Are you still writing to Gregg?" Liz asked teasingly. She held the letter up to face the sunlight and pretended to peer inside.

Laurie lunged for the envelope, stumbling across the redwood picnic table and hitting her elbow on it. "If I wanted you to see what was inside, I wouldn't have sealed it," she complained, rubbing her bruised arm.

"Calm down," said Liz, in the patient older-sister voice that always drove Laurie crazy. "I don't read other people's mail. It's just that I think it might be a good idea for you to hold off on writing to Gregg for a while." She slipped the letter into her bulging canvas shoulder bag.

"Why shouldn't I write to him?" Laurie asked, her gray eyes wide with surprise. "Gregg and I have been friends since kindergarten."

"Look, Laurie, I don't want to make you feel bad or anything, but it's time that you faced the facts. Gregg and his family moved to Connecticut over a year ago. Just last week you said that his letters are always full of news about all his new friends," Liz explained. "Gregg has a great personality, and it was probably easy for him to make a new life for himself. I guess what I'm trying to say is that he probably isn't hanging on to the past the way you are," she said, digging into the pockets of her heavy cherry-red sweater. "Have you seen my car keys?" Liz asked anxiously.

"I think they're in the house on the kitchen table," Laurie replied. She wished she could ignore everything that her sister had just said, but Liz's words really bothered her. She sud-

2

denly had the urge to start up the conversation all over again.

Laurie turned back toward her sister, who was rummaging through her bag. "You don't understand my relationship with Gregg at all, Liz," she said defensively. "When you live next door to someone for most of your life, you become a lot more than just friends."

"But you don't live next door to each other anymore," Liz said softly. "And you're both grown-up now. Don't you think it's about time for you to put Gregg in the past, where he belongs?"

"I can't," Laurie replied honestly. "Gregg's too important to forget about."

"Well, don't say I didn't warn you," Liz said with a sigh. "But I promise I'll mail your letter. Will you remember to tell Mom that I won't be home for dinner tonight? I've got an English paper due soon, and I've still got tons of research to do, so I'll be at the library for a couple of hours. I'll just grab a hamburger or something on the way home." She ran into the house to retrieve her car keys, grumbling something about college turning out to be more work than she had anticipated. Laurie heard the front door slam and then heard her sister's footsteps on the driveway.

Laurie sank down onto the cushioned chaise longue. The late-afternoon air was very still, and she could hear a dog barking far off in the distance. Suddenly Laurie was overcome by a wave of loneliness. The gnawing ache had started long before Gregg actually moved away. Just thinking about his not being around anymore was enough to make Laurie feel as if she had been abandoned on a desert island. Losing Gregg had been like losing a part of herself. He had always been her best friend, the one person she could count on to be there for her no matter what. They had shared so many experiences that most of Laurie's memories included Gregg in one way or another.

In their first year of junior high, for instance, Gregg had suddenly discovered fishing, and he wouldn't rest until he had persuaded Laurie to try it as well. Months went by before she dared to bait her own hook with the live, wiggling worms Gregg gave her. But eventually she overcame her queasiness because she didn't want to disappoint him. After a few seasons of practice, and many mishaps, they even won a fishing competition together. They were awarded an engraved wooden plaque for catching the largest bass, and Gregg had gallantly insisted that Laurie keep their prize; it was still hanging on her bedroom wall.

Then, there were all the writing competitions that Laurie had entered. She had never actually won first prize, but she *had* gotten honorable mention for a poem once. Gregg had taken her out for an ice-cream sundae to celebrate, and he seemed even happier and prouder than Laurie herself. He had made her promise she would give him an autographed copy of her first published book.

So, Laurie couldn't pretend that Gregg didn't exist anymore simply because he had moved to southern Connecticut. He was still the most wonderful boy she had ever met. None of the boys at school compared with him, and in her opinion, she and Gregg had shared too much not to continue a friendship.

At first Gregg's letters had been like hers, filled with the memories of good times they had shared and complaints about how much he missed their hometown of Skylar and Laurie. But gradually the tone of his letters had changed, and he became very enthusiastic about New Brunswick High and all the new friends he was making there. Lately Gregg had even become interested in school politics, something he had never discussed with Laurie before. Whenever she reread his letters, Laurie could feel a cold knot forming in the pit of her stomach. She was glad Gregg was happy with his new life, but she couldn't help worrying that he might be slipping away from her. And what frustrated her the most was that there was nothing she could do about it.

Laurie sat up suddenly, startled from her thoughts as she heard a car pull into the driveway. She peered over the patio railing in time to see her mother's station wagon glide into the garage. Laurie instantly sprang up to set three places at the picnic table. She had promised her mother that she would have everything ready for dinner that night, but because of her daydreaming, she had lost all track of time.

"Hi, honey," Mrs. Raymond said, greeting her daughter. "I hope you haven't started dinner yet. Dad and I stopped off at the market on our way from the station to buy some beautiful steaks."

"I thought we were just barbecuing hamburgers," said Laurie in surprise. "Is this a special occasion or something?" she asked, looking from one parent to the other. Mrs. Raymond was smiling mysteriously.

"As a matter of fact, it is," Mr. Raymond replied. He loosened his tie and settled into the empty chaise longue. "I've got some good news for you, Laurie. Something that I think you in particular will be delighted to hear," he added, winking at his wife.

Laurie couldn't imagine what her father was talking about, but it was obvious that her parents were sharing some sort of secret. "What is it, Dad?" she asked. "Did you get the raise or something?" She knew that her father, who happened to work for the same company as Gregg's father, was being considered for a promotion right then. Maybe that was it. Laurie hoped that her father would finally receive the recognition he deserved.

"Actually, I did get the raise. But there are also some fringe benefits that go along with it," Mr. Raymond replied with a grin.

"Go on, Paul, tell her," Mrs. Raymond urged, perching on the edge of the chaise.

"All right, I'll end the suspense," he agreed. "Laurie, I've finally received my promotion, and I've been transferred to the company's office in Connecticut. We'll be relocating to New Brunswick as soon as we can make the necessary arrangements," he added. "Probably by mid-October."

Laurie was completely stunned. It took several moments for her father's words to sink in.

"We'll be living in the same town as the Crawfords, honey," said Mrs. Raymond enthusiastically. "The last time I heard from Sarah Crawford, she told me how much they all love New Brunswick. Apparently the town has a lovely old-fashioned village square and antique shops everywhere, and she and Bill even bought a home that dates back to the 1820s. Doesn't that sound wonderful? I can hardly wait to start house hunting." Mrs. Raymond's eyes were glowing with anticipation.

"And Sarah also told me how much Gregg is enjoying his new school," she continued. "He's made so many friends, Laurie. And I'm sure that you'll love it in New Brunswick, too." Mrs. Raymond stood up to retrieve the bag of groceries she had left on the flagstone patio.

Laurie was so happy, she couldn't stop smiling. It was the very best present anyone could have given her, and she couldn't believe her luck. Once Gregg saw her again, everything would be the way it always had been.

"I'm going to roast some corn on the cob, too," said Mrs. Raymond as she and her husband started into the house. Mrs. Raymond stopped at the door. "Where's Liz?" she asked, turning around.

"She's studying late at the library tonight," Laurie replied. In her excitement she had forgotten all about Liz's message. It seemed as if the conversation with her sister had taken place ages ago, when really only a short time had passed. An hour ago she had been missing Gregg desperately, but now she knew they would be together again soon.

"Then it's just the three of us tonight," said Mrs. Raymond, interrupting her daughter's thoughts. "Well, you've got plenty of time before dinner will be ready, honey."

From the patio Laurie could hear only snatches of her parents' conversation inside the house. Their voices sounded very far away as she relaxed, enjoying the balmy September breeze. Everything about the early evening seemed magical now, and Laurie wished that she could capture those moments forever. She knew she was on the brink of an exciting new adventure, and she couldn't wait to actually plunge into it.

Even though she would be moving to a new state, Laurie felt as if she would be going home. Happiness and security were wherever Gregg was, and soon she would be with him again. It was almost too wonderful to believe that her family could be settled in New Brunswick as early as mid-October.

Laurie's first impulse was to run upstairs and call Gregg, but she knew her parents didn't like her calling long-distance. Then she considered writing him a long letter to tell him her news, but she finally decided against it. It would be much more fun to surprise him. Gregg had always loved surprises.

In the sixth grade Laurie had wanted to buy Gregg an extra-special birthday present. She didn't have much money, but finally she had thought of a terrific idea. Gregg's birthday fell in January, and she remembered seeing an old wooden toboggan that had been sitting in the Raymonds' shed for years. Gregg loved sledding, and Laurie had decided she would restore the toboggan and give it to him. After dragging the sled down to their basement, Laurie had worked on it every spare moment she had. The tricky part had been making sure that Gregg didn't walk in before she was ready to unveil her surprise. Laurie had sanded the sled until her arms ached, and then she had painted the wooden slats bright red. When she had finished, the sled was beautiful and Gregg had been very impressed. They had fun using that toboggan for years afterward. And the funny thing was, she had gotten as much enjoyment out of restoring the toboggan as Gregg had gotten out of using it.

Liz would probably have said that those days were long gone, but Laurie didn't care. Now, there would be more wonderful memories to make together in the future. She knew that she needed her family's help to keep their move a secret from Gregg, but she was sure that everyone would cooperate. She hoped that her mother hadn't said anything to Mrs. Crawford yet.

Laurie walked inside and climbed the stairs to her bedroom. The room had always been hers, and she looked around nostalgically. She would miss Skylar and her friends, of course, but it would definitely be worth moving to be with Gregg again. Laurie walked across the thick blue carpeting to her desk and picked up the yellow legal pad that lay on top of it. She reread the last few lines of the poem she had been working on earlier and then sat down to finish it, the words flowing easily from her pen. Laurie loved to write, and it was something she did well. At special times like this she liked to work on her secret poetry project—secret from everyone but Gregg.

Chapter Two

"I have absolutely nothing to wear," Laurie moaned, delving into her closet once again. She stared forlornly at the blue-and-white-flowered blouse she had pulled off a hanger.

"What on earth are you talking about?" Liz asked, leaning against the door frame of Laurie's bedroom in their new house. "You've got plenty of clothes. I never realized that you cared that much about how you looked."

"Well, I didn't before, but today's special. I'm going to see Gregg for the first time in months," she replied. Laurie could feel tears of nervousness and frustration burning her eyes. Absolutely nothing had gone right that morning. She had gotten up extra early to wash her long brown hair, only to discover that they were all out of conditioner. Then the zipper on her favorite corduroy skirt had broken, and now she couldn't find anything else to wear.

"Listen, I'll help you, OK? Just calm down," said Liz. "I've got plenty of time to hang around here helping you, since I won't be able to start at my new college until next semester."

Laurie forgot her own troubles for a second and turned to face her sister. "Do you think you'll like the new school?"

"Yes," said Liz. "It looked great, and there are lots of cute guys," she added, stepping farther into the room. "Here, let me help you put something together," she offered.

Laurie hadn't had time to decorate her room yet, and the walls were still covered with the original green- and gold-striped wallpaper. The first item of importance on her list of things to do—before she could even *think* of decorating—was to see Gregg, and she wanted to look her very best when she did. She thought about how hard it had been to put off their reunion. Only by enlisting Gregg's parents, as well as her own, to help had she been able

14

to avoid seeing him for the few days they had been in Connecticut. Laurie was determined to make their first meeting at school a total surprise.

"Why don't you just wear a pair of jeans and a sweater?" Liz suggested, lifting a warm yellow pullover form Laurie's dresser drawer. "Most of the kids will probably be dressed casually."

"I don't know," said Laurie, shaking her head uncertainly. "I was counting on wearing my dark blue skirt, but the zipper jammed. That outfit would have been a little more special than plain old jeans." She slipped carefully into the skirt and tugged gently at the zipper, trying to pull it free.

"Laurie, what on earth are you getting so dressed up for? You want to fit in here, not stand out." Liz ran her fingers through her short hair, which was the same shade of brown as her sister's. The two girls looked enough alike to be twins, but Liz was two years older and four inches taller than Laurie, who was a petite five-foot-one.

Their personalities, however, couldn't have been more different. Liz never hesitated to express her opinion on any issue; she was as outgoing as Laurie was shy.

"Oh, Liz, I want to look perfect for Gregg, and he's used to seeing me in sweaters and skirts at school. I don't want to wear anything he might not like," Laurie insisted.

"OK, if that's the way you feel. I can pin the zipper right here," said Liz, maneuvering a safety pin into the folds of the skirt so that it couldn't be seen. "There, now you're all set. And if you wear your long white sweater over the skirt, you can be sure that no one will even notice the zipper." Liz smiled in satisfaction as Laurie pulled the V-neck sweater over her head and smoothed it into place.

"Liz, you're terrific. I take back all the horrible things I've ever said to you." At least one of her problems had been solved, Laurie thought. She picked up her hairbrush, ran it quickly through her silky hair, and then applied some peach-colored lip gloss.

"Want to borrow some of my makeup?" Liz offered.

Laurie shook her head. "No thanks. Gregg's not used to seeing me in makeup. I want to look exactly the same as I did before," she explained, stepping back from the mirror for a last-minute inspection.

"You look great, Laurie, really. But don't expect everything to have stayed the same between you and Gregg, OK? People *do* change, you know," warned Liz with a worried frown.

"Not Gregg." Laurie's voice was confident. "I'm sure that nothing will have changed between us."

Liz smiled at her younger sister. "How about a ride to school," she offered. "Unless you're dying to ride the school bus."

Laurie smiled gratefully. "Thanks, Liz. I was really dreading having to take the bus on my first day," she admitted.

The short ride to New Brunswick High went all too quickly, and Laurie could feel the butterflies dancing in her stomach as Liz pulled the car up to the front entrance. The modern, sprawling building was completely different from the traditional-looking high school she had gone to in Skylar. Everything seemed so much larger and brighter. A huge expanse of emerald-green lawn circled the building on three sides, and the sports fields appeared to stretch on endlessly. The parking lot was already filled with cars, and Laurie realized with a shock that a lot more kids drove their own cars to school here than back home. For a minute she almost panicked, but then she smiled confidently to herself. With Gregg by her side, she'd have no problem adjusting to New Brunswick High.

"Want some help with registration?" Liz asked, sensing Laurie's nervousness.

Laurie shook her head. "No, thanks. I'm a big girl now, remember?" she added, smiling slightly. She knew that her words weren't very convincing, but they were the best she could manage at the moment. She lifted her bag off the seat, climbed out of the car, and waved goodbye to her sister. Then, she stood for a long moment, watching as the bright yellow car vanished around the corner.

Well, this is it. Sink or swim, Laurie decided. She pushed open the wide glass doors to the building and slowly followed a large group of kids as they sauntered down the long corridor.

No one paid the slightest bit of attention to Laurie as she looked around trying to locate the school's administration office. Although she was surrounded by a mob of kids her own age, there didn't really seem to be anybody whom she could stop to ask directions. They were all involved in conversations with their friends or trying to scribble last-minute homework assignments. Laurie was begin-

18

ning to feel as if she had landed on an alien planet and was totally invisible.

Every direction in which she turned seemed to be the wrong one. The halls were endless, and Laurie couldn't stop the waves of panic that were beginning to wash over her. If she didn't find the office soon, she was going to miss her first class. Even though most of the paperwork for her registration had been completed by mail and she had already received her schedule card, Laurie was told to check in with the office as soon as she arrived.

Hearing footsteps behind her, Laurie turned to face a girl wearing calf-length jeans and a body-hugging white t-shirt. The girl wasn't looking where she was going and almost crashed right into Laurie. "Excuse me, but could you tell me where the registration office is?" Laurie asked.

Startled, the girl stared at Laurie from behind a pair of dark glasses, then shrugged. "Down this hall, turn right, and take your first left," she said, continuing on her way. Before Laurie had a chance to double-check the directions, the girl had vanished. Laurie began to wonder if maybe she *should* have called Gregg as soon as she arrived in Connecticut. Everything would have been so much easier with him to help her.

Laurie finally reached the office, and everything went smoothly enough, but by the time she was allowed to leave, she only had time for one class before lunch. Unfortunately, that class was French, one of her least favorite subjects. The instructor, Monsieur Jabon, was less than friendly, and he immediately handed Laurie a thick textbook and a photocopied list of back assignments. His cool tone made her feel more like an unwelcome intruder than a student.

Laurie searched frantically for Gregg after her class, but she didn't have any luck in finding him. She would have to make it through lunch on her own.

It was not going to be easy, she decided, picking up an orange plastic tray and sliding it along the chrome bars of the hot-lunch line. Spaghetti and meatballs was the special of the day, and Laurie wrinkled her nose at the pungent aroma. Her stomach was too tied up in knots to handle anything that heavy, so she picked up a plain tossed salad and a serving of strawberry Jell-O. After paying the cashier, she stepped forward hesitantly, searching for an empty seat. They were few and far between, but she finally spotted one and approached the table timidly.

"Sorry, but we're saving that seat for a friend," said one girl as Laurie put down her tray. She picked it up again and backed off as though she had been slapped.

"Is this seat taken?" she asked at another table, where a bunch of girls were having a lively discussion. They looked at one another, and then a heavily made-up brown-haired girl said, "I'm expecting my boyfriend any minute, so I've got to keep that seat open. Sorry."

Holding her tray firmly, Laurie moved several feet away. She felt the hot sting of tears burning her eyes and was afraid she wouldn't be able to keep them back much longer. Gregg had made everyone sound so nice and friendly in his letters, and she could hardly believe that this was the same school he had written about. Laurie could tell that it was going to be even harder than she had thought to be the new girl in such a large school. She was just about to put down her tray and leave—when she saw him. At first she couldn't believe that it was really Gregg. She had dreamed about seeing him for so long that it seemed impossible that the moment had really come.

He was even more handsome than she had remembered. Her heart melted as she watched him flick a wayward lock of dark wavy hair off his forehead. His familiar dimples flashed as he smiled at something, and then she heard him laugh out loud. Laurie felt a physical ache at the familiar, comforting sound of his laughter.

Everyone and everything else in the room suddenly seemed to disappear. Gone were the noisy cafeteria conversation and the clatter of dishes on trays. Laurie saw only Gregg. On impulse she put down her tray and rushed forward, stopping only inches away from him.

"Gregg!" His name seemed to catch in her throat, and her voice was little more than a hoarse whisper. Laurie had to call to him again before he turned and saw her. It was almost worth the months of missing him, as she watched his deep brown eyes widen in shock.

"Laurie? Laurie, is it really you?" he cried, throwing his arms around her. He caught her in such a tight hug that she could hardly breathe. Then, he stepped back and caught her hands tightly in his own. "I can't believe it," he said, grinning broadly. "What are you doing here?"

"My dad transferred to New Brunswick, too," Laurie explained. "This is my first day of school." Her voice sounded strange to her ears, and all she could think of was the warm pressure of Gregg's hands on her own.

He leaned forward to give her another hug. "This is absolutely *incredible*. I still can't believe it," he repeated.

"Hey, Crawford, who's your friend?"

Gregg turned to the tall boy who stood beside him. "This is an old friend of mine from Skylar, Bob. I'd like you to meet Laurie Raymond," he said.

Slowly Laurie became aware that Gregg was with a whole group of kids. She was amazed that she hadn't noticed them sooner.

"It's nice to meet you, Laurie," said Bob, scrutinizing her closely.

Laurie felt very uncomfortable as five pairs of strange eyes focused on her. But these were the friends Gregg had written about, and she wanted to make a good impression.

Their names seemed vaguely familiar to Laurie as Gregg introduced them one after another to her. There was Jason, who was very muscular, and Laurie remembered that he was on New Brunswick High's football team. And the three girls with Gregg were all very pretty, particularly Nicole. She had long blond hair and eyes that were an unusual shade of aqua blue. After smiling her greetings, Laurie quickly turned her attention back to Gregg.

"That's our usual table over there," he said, nodding toward the far corner of the cafeteria. "Come, sit with us." Gregg was still grinning from ear to ear.

Laurie nodded. "Thanks, I'd like to," she replied. If only everyone else would vanish so she could be alone with Gregg, she thought as she collected her tray. She had imagined this first meeting with him thousands of times, but her dreams had never included a group of his friends. She decided she'd just have to smile and make the best of it. After all, they'd have plenty of time alone later on.

"How come you didn't tell me you were moving to Connecticut in any of your letters?" asked Gregg as he took the seat next to Laurie's.

"It all happened so quickly," she answered. "Besides, I wanted to surprise you."

Gregg laughed. "Like you did with that old red toboggan?" he asked, smiling. He told the group about the toboggan that she had refinished for him so long ago.

"That thing had incredible speed," he

said with a fond smile.
had it."

"My dad has a skimobile.
the fairways at the country cl
Nicole. "You feel just like you'r
she added with an adoring smile

Laurie's heart skipped a beat as s......ched
the girl. It was obvious from the way she
looked at him that Nicole was interested in
Gregg. Whether or not he returned her feelings, Laurie couldn't tell. Gregg seemed to be
equally friendly to everyone in the group.

"Are you on a diet, Laurie?" asked Nicole,
glancing at Laurie's plain salad.

Laurie was surprised by the attractive blond
girl's interest in her lunch. The idea of a diet
had never occurred to her, as she had always
felt comfortable with her height and her
weight. She squirmed in her seat and put
down the spoonful of strawberry Jell-O she
had been about to eat. "No, not really. I guess
I was just too nervous to eat much lunch
today," she replied, noting Nicole's slender
figure. Maybe taking off a few pounds wouldn't
hurt, Laurie thought.

"Well, there's nothing to be nervous about.
Right, guys?" said Gregg heartily. "New Brunswick High is a terrific school."

part of your campaign speech, _____?" asked Jason with a teasing grin. "____ it is, you've already got my vote."

"Mine, too," added Nicole, reaching out to squeeze Gregg's hand across the lunch table. "You're going to be the next class president for sure."

Laurie stared at Gregg in amazement. "Are you running for class president?" she asked. Gregg had mentioned an interest in school politics once or twice in his letters, but she had never imagined that he would become so involved.

"Oh, absolutely," said Heather, a pretty, delicate-looking girl with huge green eyes. "Not only is he campaigning, he's a shoo-in."

"Gregg, I've sketched a few more publicity posters I'd like you to take a look at," said Nicole. "If you like them, my dad can have them copied at his office. We'll hang them all over school."

"Thanks, Nicole. I'm sure they're terrific," Gregg replied gratefully.

Laurie couldn't stop the tide of hurt that washed over her as she watched Gregg and Nicole together. She had never seen him with another girl, and the experience was far from pleasant.

"Hey, I've got a great idea, Crawford. When I announce the day's activities over the PA system tomorrow morning, I'll give you a plug," offered Bob.

"No wonder I'm getting more publicity than my opponent," said Gregg, laughing. "You guys are a great team."

Laurie watched as everyone at the table beamed. Gregg definitely had a way with people. It was a special gift, one she had always sensed in him. He had just never developed it in Skylar. He had always been more open and outgoing than she, of course, but he seemed to have really made a place for himself at New Brunswick High. Laurie was happy for him, but in Skylar, she had at least been an accepted member of their group of friends. Here, she was an outsider.

Suddenly feeling like a stranger with Gregg, she said hesitantly, "Gregg, do you remember when we entered that roller-skating contest?" Her cheeks grew warm with embarrassment as she realized that everyone's attention was suddenly focused on her.

"Sure," said Gregg. "We were terrific, weren't we? Maybe not first-prize material, but definitely worth watching. We'd worked up a pretty

27

good routine. Think you could remember any of the steps?"

Laurie nodded. Gregg always made her feel so much better about everything. "I remember all of them," she said. "We *did* practice almost every afternoon for a whole month."

"How about testing your memory this weekend?" Gregg suggested. His brown eyes twinkled with laughter. "You can't back out now, Laurie," he warned, nudging her with his elbow.

Backing out was the last thing on Laurie's mind. She was thrilled by Gregg's invitation because she hadn't been sure they'd actually start to date.

"I'd love to go, Gregg," she said with a warm smile. "I'll have to rent a pair of skates, though. I've outgrown my old ones since our skating days."

"That's OK. I don't think any of us have skates of our own. How about it, guys?"

Laurie was stunned. Was he including all these people in their date? She thought that they'd be going out alone, not with a crowd. Her heart sank as she realized she wouldn't have Gregg all to herself.

"I don't have any skates either, Laurie,"

said Amy. She was a pretty girl with an incredibly long mane of thick brown curls.

"Well, I've got a pair," chirped Nicole brightly. "I love to skate," she added, throwing a triumphant look in Laurie's direction.

Laurie glanced at Gregg, but he was too excited about his idea to notice the growing rivalry between her and Nicole. "Great, then it's a date," he was saying. "Saturday night at the rink."

Laurie forced a smile. At least she was near Gregg again, she reminded herself. They'd have plenty of time to be alone later on. And in the meantime she'd have a chance to really get to know his friends.

Chapter Three

"OK, I'm all out of suggestions," Liz grumbled in exasperation as she sank down onto the one uncluttered corner of Laurie's bed. "Look at this mess. Every piece of clothing you own must be lying here somewhere," she said, waving toward the piles of shirts and pants that were strewn all around the bedroom.

"Liz, you can't give up on me now," pleaded Laurie. "Gregg will be picking me up soon, and I still don't know what to wear." She stared unhappily at the few blouses and sweaters still hanging in her almost bare closet.

"Laurie, I've never seen you like this. You're always saying that you and Gregg are so close and very comfortable together. What's happened to change all that?" Liz asked, her gray eyes clouded with concern.

"Gregg is still my best friend," insisted Laurie. What she didn't say was that she wasn't sure how *he* felt about *her* anymore. "It's just that this will be the first time we've gone out together in over a year, and I want to wear something special," she explained.

"Are you sure his friends don't have something to do with your being so upset?" Liz prodded gently.

"Maybe," admitted Laurie with a shrug. "I guess I didn't expect Gregg to be part of such a sophisticated crowd."

Laurie sighed wistfully. She had spent her first week at her new school trying to catch up on assignments and become better acquainted with Gregg's friends. Both tasks had been far from easy. She had grown up knowing everyone in Skylar, and being the new girl in town was more difficult than she had imagined.

"I tried to warn you that things might have changed. Gregg's very popular. You can't really blame him for having lots of friends or running for class president," said Liz.

Laurie nodded. Her sister was right. "I know, and I'm really going to try hard to fit in," she promised. "That's why I have to find the perfect thing to wear tonight." She was sure that Nicole would look absolutely gorgeous, and she didn't want to look like a total nerd in comparison.

"I'd lend you my new stirrup pants, but they'd hang down to your toes," said Liz with a laugh. "Look, you always used to wear jeans whenever you and Gregg went skating in Skylar. Do you really think he'll be expecting to find you dressed in sequins and lace?"

"I don't know what he's expecting, Liz. That's the problem. All the girls in Gregg's crowd are really popular. They have the most terrific clothes, and I haven't bought anything new in ages," said Laurie, frantically searching through her dresser drawers. Finally she pulled out a pair of jeans. "These are my best ones. Do you really think they'll be OK?"

"How can anyone go wrong wearing jeans and a sweater?" asked Liz. "Don't worry about what the other girls will be wearing. They'll probably be dressed the same way as you, anyway."

"OK, you win," said Laurie, pulling on a yellow-and-white-striped turtleneck sweater. After she had finally gotten her head through the tight neckline, her hair was flying in all directions. "Look at me," she moaned, staring into the full-length mirror on her closet door. "This static electricity makes me look like the Bride of Frankenstein."

"Don't panic, Laur. I've got an idea," Liz said as she reached for Laurie's brush and gently eased the bristles through her sister's shiny hair. She then fished a pair of blue barrettes from the glass tray on top of Laurie's dresser and fastened them, sweeping the front section of Laurie's hair up and away from her forehead to highlight her pretty gray eyes.

"There. You look wonderful," she said with a smile of satisfaction.

"I look like a ten-year-old," complained Laurie. "But at least it's neat. Thanks."

"Wait just a minute," said Liz. She darted out of the bedroom and returned with a new, hand-painted wooden bracelet. "Here, put this on," she ordered, stepping back to admire the effect. "Perfect. You look absolutely terrific, and it doesn't matter what that girl, Nicole, is wearing."

Laurie laughed. "Sometimes I'm really glad that you're my sister."

Liz threw a pillow at her. "What do you mean *sometimes*?" she asked teasingly.

"Well, most of the time I'm glad to have you around," Laurie replied, throwing the pillow back at Liz.

She jumped as the doorbell rang downstairs, feeling her throat go as dry as cotton and her heart begin to pump crazily. "That's Gregg," she whispered in a panic.

"You mean the same Gregg you lived next door to for about eleven years?" asked Liz.

Laurie nodded. "I keep trying to remind myself of that," she said, frowning nervously.

"Come on. You'll be fine," Liz promised. Putting her arm around Laurie's shoulders, she propelled her sister toward the stairs.

The doorbell rang again, and Laurie could hear her mother open the door and welcome Gregg. From the laughter in the front hallway, she knew they were enjoying their reunion. The Raymonds had always considered Gregg an adopted member of their family.

"Laurie, Gregg's here, honey," called her mother.

Laurie took a deep breath, gave Liz's hand a quick squeeze for support, and headed down the stairs. She was surprised to see that Gregg was alone. She had been expecting him to be surrounded by a crowd of friends, and now her hopes soared. Maybe they had all decided not to come. Or better yet, maybe Gregg had decided he'd rather be alone with her.

"Hi, Gregg," she said with a smile. He looked so handsome in his jeans and fisherman knit sweater.

"Hi, Laurie. I was just telling your mom how great it is to have you all here in Connecticut. It kind of reminds me of old times."

Laurie nodded. "I know," she said, pleased that Gregg felt the same way she did.

"I'd love to stay and visit awhile, Mrs. Raymond, but Nicole and Jason are waiting for us in the car. The rest of the gang's going to meet us at the rink," he added, holding Laurie's jacket as she slipped her arms into the sleeves.

Laurie felt her heart drop a little. So they'd be spending the evening with his friends after all. Well, she'd just have to wait until their next date to be alone with him. She hoped her disappointment didn't show too much.

Laurie shivered as they stepped out into

the chilly October night, and Gregg put his arm around her shoulders the way he had dozens of times before. Laurie was totally unprepared for the shock of electricity that raced through her body at his casual touch. How could a boy she had known most of her life make her feel that way?

"Are you cold?" he asked, concerned.

Laurie shook her head. "Well, maybe just a little," she said with a smile, pleased that he had asked.

"Come on, you guys," called Nicole impatiently as she rolled down the car window. "By the time we get to the rink, it'll be mobbed."

"That makes it more fun," said Gregg, laughing. He held the passenger door of his car open for Laurie before getting in on the driver's side. "You have to maneuver in between all the other skaters without crashing into them."

"Well, I'm not even going to fall down once," said Nicole. "Let's just see if you guys can match that," she said as a challenge.

"You're on," said Gregg. "Laurie and I were a great skating team," he added. "So whoever loses has to spring for lunch in the school cafeteria."

"Ugh," said Jason with a shudder. "Couldn't you make it a little more appealing?" The others laughed.

"Gregg," Nicole broke in, "I've been taking a poll at school. It looks like you're a sure bet to be elected class president." She reached forward to touch Gregg's shoulder lightly.

"You can't count the votes until they're all in," replied Gregg matter-of-factly. "Ken Roberts is a strong opponent; he's got lots of people behind him, too. Besides, a candidate has to convince the majority of voters that his ideas and goals are worthwhile."

"See what I mean?" said Nicole proudly. "You can make speeches when you're not even trying. You're definitely the best man for the job."

Laurie squirmed in her seat uncomfortably. Nicole sounded as if she owned Gregg, or wanted to. And he was so involved with his new friends that she was beginning to wonder if she'd *ever* get to see him alone. If he won the election, he'd be even more popular. Well, she'd just have to keep reminding him of the great times they had shared. This skating party was a perfect opportunity. Once they got onto the rink, he'd remember how much fun they had always had together.

"OK, gang, all out for the Roller Derby," said Gregg, pulling his car into a space in the parking lot.

"We're going to have one fantastic time," said Nicole confidently.

Inside, Gregg rented skates for himself and Laurie and then helped Laurie lace hers. "It sure feels strange to be wearing these again," he said as he took her hand and tottered across the floor to the skating area.

Laurie nodded. "I know," she said. "Maybe it'll all come back to us as soon as we get warmed up," she added hopefully.

The floor was crowded with skaters. Laurie noticed that many of the kids waved to Gregg or said hello as they passed.

"OK, Crawford. Let's see what you've got," called Bob, skating toward them with Heather in tow. Nicole, Jason, and Amy soon joined them, and Laurie realized that the group had been evenly matched, boys to girls, until she'd shown up. Suddenly she felt like even more of a fifth wheel. She watched as Nicole twirled gracefully, showing off her figure in a flashy silver-and-white miniskirt and a clinging silver-weave sweater. Laurie felt ordinary by comparison.

"OK, Laurie, let's show them we weren't

kidding," challenged Gregg. He spoke very loudly to make his voice heard over the music that vibrated from every corner of the cavernous room.

Laurie took a deep breath and prayed she'd remember all the steps to their old routine. She felt like an actress about to go onstage, with Gregg's friends as her audience. She was so nervous that she couldn't concentrate on her skating, and she kept glancing around the rink to see what Nicole was doing. When she finally spotted the other girl, Laurie almost lost her balance. Nicole was obviously a trained dancer as well as an excellent skater. Laurie had never seen anyone move so gracefully. Nicole glided as smoothly as a swan, Laurie thought dismally as she stumbled against Gregg's side.

"Relax, Laurie. It's just for fun," said Gregg. He seemed to sense her tenseness, and she felt her cheeks grow warm as she realized that she had a death grip on his hands. No wonder he wanted her to get a hold of herself.

"You're doing fine," he said encouragingly as he led her through their old routine. Gregg was a terrific skater, and he remembered every step of the number. It was easy to follow his lead, and Laurie gradually relaxed as they matched their steps and rhythm.

"Way to go, guys," called Jason as he skated by with Amy.

Laurie realized that she was smiling, and what was more, she was really enjoying herself. Not only did she love to skate, but it felt wonderful being that close to Gregg again. They skated steadily for three more songs, and then Gregg suggested they take a break.

"How about stopping for a soda?" he asked, his cheeks flushed. Laurie's heart hammered noisily as she met the gaze of his sparkling brown eyes. He was the most handsome boy she had ever known. It was hard to blame Nicole for being interested in him. *What girl wouldn't be?* she thought to herself.

"We ought to work out a new routine," said Gregg as he placed their sodas on an empty table right next to the skating floor. "We're already doing pretty well on the old one."

"OK," Laurie agreed, frowning slightly. "But I'm not as good a skater as you are." She felt comfortable sticking with the old tried-and-true routine, and she wasn't anxious to try anything different. Her doubt increased as she watched Nicole skating alone. The girl moved in perfect time with the music, as though she had rehearsed her steps thousands of times.

"Nicole's a dynamite skater, isn't she?" said Gregg, nodding toward the pretty blond girl. "But this stuff is easy for her. She's studied dance since she was a little kid. The rest of us mortals have to work harder," he said, squeezing Laurie's hand.

"Oh, Gregg. You're not going to make me skate alone, are you?" wheedled Nicole, coming to a graceful stop and leaning over the railing in front of their table.

Gregg looked questioningly at Laurie. "You don't mind, do you, Laurie?" he asked.

Laurie shook her head, amazed that he couldn't hear her heart crying out that she certainly did mind. But she knew she couldn't demand Gregg's undivided attention. After all, Nicole was one of his friends.

"No, of course not," she said, forcing a smile that she hoped looked real. "I'll watch."

"Great. I'll be back in a few minutes," he promised. Nicole reached for his hand and led him back onto the crowded rink.

Laurie hadn't realized that she was squeezing her paper cup until the cold, sticky soda poured out over the top and onto her hand. She had been completely absorbed in watching Gregg and Nicole together. They looked so professional that many of the other skaters had stopped to watch and give them more room.

Gregg swung Nicole at arm's length, and she spun like a ballerina. They continued performing, one routine after another, improvising as they went along. When the music finally ended, they returned to Laurie's table, smiling and exhausted.

"You were terrific," said Laurie sincerely. But her compliment was drowned out as the rest of the group joined them.

"You guys ought to be on TV," said Jason, giving Gregg a congratulatory slap on the back.

"The Fred Astaire and Ginger Rogers of the Roller Derby," said Nicole with a laugh, her sea-blue eyes sparkling with excitement.

"Come and try some of those new steps with me, Laurie," urged Gregg, reaching for her hand.

Laurie shook her head. "I couldn't do those, Gregg," she said with an apologetic smile. She couldn't possibly compete with Nicole's performance, and there was no point in even trying. She'd look ridiculous.

Seeing Gregg's disappointed look, Laurie

wondered if she hadn't made a mistake in refusing to try some of the skating steps. Now Gregg was unhappy. She was afraid that he might have moved ahead of her into a life where she didn't really belong. For her, their old skating routine was good enough, but it was obvious that Gregg expected more from her now. She would just have to try harder to be the sort of person he wanted her to be.

Chapter Four

"You should have tried some of those new steps," said Liz as she leaned in toward the mirror, blending a soft shade of blue shadow onto her eyelids.

"I know, but I was afraid to," Laurie admitted, sagging against the brass headboard of the twin bed. Liz had just finished decorating her bedroom in a terrific shade of peach, and Laurie loved being there. It had such a mellow, gentle feel to it, quite unlike Liz herself, who was always full of energy. She claimed that she had purposely decorated the room in a soothing color to help her wind down after a busy day.

"You can't be afraid to try new things, Laurie," Liz said philosophically, glancing at her younger sister in the mirror. "What you did in the past doesn't count. Gregg is obviously interested in what's going on now," she added, turning back to her makeup.

"Gregg's interested in Nicole," said Laurie with a dismal frown.

"There's no reason why you can't join in things just as well as she can," replied Liz. "I don't remember you being this shy in Skylar." She opened her eyes wide and brushed her lashes with dark mascara.

"There was nothing to be shy about in Skylar. I'd lived there my whole life," said Laurie with a sigh as she picked up her book bag. Liz didn't really understand what it was like to be shy since she was always so sure of herself.

Laurie glanced at her watch; it was getting very late. "I'd better get outside, or I'll miss the school bus," she said, glad to change the subject. "See you this afternoon," she called over her shoulder, racing down the stairs and out the front door.

The yellow bus arrived within minutes, rattling to a stop in front of the Raymonds' white colonial house. Laurie climbed down from the old stone wall where she had been sitting and entered the crowded bus. She took a seat next to a girl who smiled politely before turning back to the textbook that lay open in her lap. Laurie spent the twenty-minute ride staring out the window at the colorful New England foliage.

It was a beautiful fall day—most of the trees were orange and gold against a picture-book sky. Laurie's thoughts turned back to her troubles. Maybe Liz was right. Everything *had* to change eventually, just like the seasons. She should have let herself go and made an attempt to learn something new Saturday night. It was obvious that Gregg had been disappointed in her. He liked to try different things, and if she wanted to make him happy, she'd have to be a lot more outgoing. She vowed to make a fresh start that very day. She'd try her best to be friendlier to the kids in his group, even Nicole, and show Gregg that she hadn't become boring. After all, he had found her interesting enough back in Skylar. But, maybe that was because she hadn't been so insecure then. Laurie sighed. It was just that everything was so unfamiliar in Connecticut, and she wasn't sure how much she could really depend on Gregg.

The bus rumbled to a halt outside the school building, its passengers pouring out as soon as the doors swung open. Everyone was so full of energy that Laurie found she was actually smiling. She knew it was a cliché, but that day *was* going to be the first day of the rest of her life. And she was determined to make it a good one.

The morning got off to a great start. Laurie loved to write, and so she enjoyed starting the outline for her essay on *Romeo and Juliet* in the library during her study hall. The play had always intrigued her, and now, thinking of how she had felt when she and Gregg were apart, she could well imagine the anguish the young couple had gone through.

Even French class was not so awful as it had been. Monsieur Jabon's thin lips almost formed a half smile as she handed him the thick packet of make-up assignments she had spent hours laboring over on Sunday.

"*Très bien, mademoiselle,*" he said, his narrow mustache twitching nervously. "I'll be expecting the rest of your work in the near future."

Laurie nodded, hoping to avoid any unnecessary conversation with her teacher. She was certain that French was going to be one of her least favorite classes at New Brunswick High. Not only was French her worst subject, but she had absolutely no rapport with Monsieur Jabon.

She could hardly wait to see Gregg at lunch. His friends would be there, too. But this time she was determined to fit in with the crowd.

When Laurie reached the cafeteria, she saw that the group had already claimed "their" table, the one in the corner that offered the most privacy. "Hi," she said, forcing her voice to sound bright and cheerful.

Gregg looked up with a warm smile, his dimples deepening as he greeted her. "Hi, Laurie," he said. "Brown bagging it today?"

All eyes were suddenly riveted on the small paper bag that Laurie had placed on the tabletop, and she immediately felt silly for having brought her lunch from home. But she really didn't like cafeteria food, and her mother had served roast chicken the night before. The idea of a cold chicken sandwich on rye bread had been very appealing to Laurie in the safety of her own kitchen.

"Wow, I haven't brought my own lunch since

sixth grade," said Nicole, spearing a piece of lettuce with her fork.

Laurie blushed, feeling her new resolve slip away.

"I'd say that Laurie's got a pretty good idea. As a matter of fact, I wish I'd brought a sandwich myself instead of forcing down that chili dog," said Gregg.

Jason and Bob laughed, and Heather and Amy joined in. Only Nicole remained silent, her blue eyes as cold as ice.

Laurie felt better when Gregg patted the seat beside him. She slid in, trying to be as inconspicuous as possible.

"Gregg, I think we should begin planning some new campaign strategies," said Nicole, sitting up straight in her chair. She tossed her mane of blond hair so that it fell in a lustrous curtain down her back.

"What do you have in mind?" asked Gregg, giving her his full attention.

"My father has run off some fliers for us. You know, the ones that say 'Gregg Crawford, New Brunswick's Number One Choice,' " she said. "Well, I thought I'd hand them out after school. Corner kids in the parking lot before they leave for the day."

Gregg laughed. "You get an *A* for effort. If I

ever run for the U.S. Senate, you can be my campaign adviser," he added with a grin.

Laurie's heart skipped a beat and then started up again at double time. She had to give Nicole credit for always managing to be the center of attention whenever the group was together. Anxious to join the conversation, she said the first thing that popped into her head. "Remember when Claire Hutchinson was running for student council in Skylar, and we made signs and marched around the school grounds for hours?"

Gregg looked puzzled for a moment and then smiled. "Oh, yeah. I do remember that," he said, nodding thoughtfully. "We walked around with sandwich boards for weeks. And as I remember it, Claire turned out to be a pretty decent council president. We did accomplish a few good things at our old alma mater."

Laurie smiled, finally beginning to feel as if she were part of the group.

"Hey, Laurie," said Gregg suddenly, his face lighting up with enthusiasm. "How about helping Nicole hand out some fliers for my campaign?"

Laurie was startled from her thoughts. Gregg was asking for her help, and there was no way she could refuse him. But she dreaded having to face so many kids. She hadn't exactly made a lot of friends yet, and the idea of approaching total strangers wasn't very appealing.

"You know, you should really get involved in some activities here," said Gregg. "This is a super school, Laurie. All you've got to do is try," he said with an encouraging smile. When Laurie still looked doubtful, he continued, "There are tons of different kinds of groups and clubs. I'm in the Drama club and the Young Executives Club."

Amy nodded, her long brown curls bobbing enthusiastically. "I'm on the cheerleading squad, Laurie. You might want to try out for that next year."

"And, your assistance on the football team would be greatly appreciated," added Jason with a teasing wink.

Laurie smiled at their suggestions. It was nice of Amy to offer, but Laurie knew she wasn't the cheerleader type.

"Thanks for your suggestion, Amy," she said. "But I think I'll start with something a little simpler. Where do I pick up the fliers, Nicole?" she asked, putting as much enthusiasm into her voice as she could manage.

Nicole didn't look thrilled to have Laurie's help. "Meet me in the front of the parking lot after school," she said shortly, applying a fresh coat of lipstick as she gazed into her compact. "And be prepared to work hard. I've got tons of fliers to hand out," she added smugly, smiling coyly at Gregg.

But Gregg's attention was focused on Laurie, and he said loyally, "You don't have to worry about Laurie, Nicole. You couldn't have a harder worker on your team."

Laurie had trouble concentrating on her schoolwork for the remainder of the day. Luckily her history teacher gave a lecture that required very little class participation, and Laurie spent most of the forty-five-minute period worrying about how she was going to distribute all of Nicole's fliers. *Don't think of them as Nicole's,* she reprimanded herself. After all, they were really for Gregg, and there wasn't anything she wouldn't do for him. Besides, Laurie had just promised herself she'd get involved in school activities. Here was the perfect opportunity to act on her resolution.

As the final bell of the day echoed in the long hallway, Laurie closed her locker door and headed toward the front parking lot. It was easy to spot Nicole, her blond hair flying in the crisp breeze. Laurie watched as the girl confidently approached one student after another, offering a bright smile and a flyer with ease. She seemed to know just about everyone, which didn't really surprise Laurie at all. Nicole was the type of girl who made it her business to be well known.

"Oh, here you are," said Nicole coldly. "I was beginning to wonder if you were really going to show up."

Laurie could feel her cheeks flaming with embarrassment and anger. "Sorry I'm late," she said quietly, wishing she had the courage to tell Nicole off. She was only there to help Gregg, and she didn't relish the idea of spending time with Nicole.

"Well, as long as you're around, you might as well get started," said Nicole briskly, handing Laurie a thick stack of brightly colored fliers.

"What should I do with them?" asked Laurie, overwhelmed at the prospect of distributing so many.

Nicole sighed, rolling her blue eyes in exasperation. "What do you think you're supposed to do with them?" she asked. "Just hand them out to people and tell them Gregg Crawford will be the best class president New

Brunswick High has ever had." Nicole turned quickly back to work, leaving Laurie on her own.

Laurie walked to the other school entrance to avoid approaching the kids who had already received fliers from Nicole. *OK*, she said to herself firmly. *This is really simple. Just walk up to someone and hand him a flier.* Even after her own little pep talk, however, it took several minutes to muster enough courage to act.

As an attractive red-haired girl wearing a cheerleader's uniform came bounding down the steps, Laurie stepped up quickly and thrust a flier toward the girl. "Gregg Crawford—"

"Sorry," called the girl, barely hesitating as she grabbed the flier from Laurie's hand. "I'm late for practice."

Laurie watched ruefully as the girl dropped the flier on her way through the parking lot. *Well, that didn't go too well*, she thought. But she was still determined to make her mission a success. After all, Gregg was depending on her. Next, Laurie approached a group of kids piling into an old blue car. "Here," she said, handing out the fliers before the car could pull away. "Gregg Crawford is—"

"Absolutely gorgeous," finished one of the girls with a giggle. A boy in the backseat folded his flier into a paper airplane and sailed it out the car window as the car pulled away with screeching tires.

Laurie hadn't realized that she had been holding her breath until she let out a deep sigh. This was turning out to be even more difficult than she had imagined. She looked over her shoulder to see if Nicole was watching her progress, or the lack of it. Fortunately, the blond girl was standing on the other side of the parking lot, surrounded by a large group of people. Laurie glanced down at her stack of fliers. There were so many of them; she'd *never* be able to hand them all out this way. She just couldn't deal with total strangers, and she felt particularly uncomfortable trying to get their attention. She scanned the parking lot briefly, an idea forming in her mind. She had the perfect answer to her problem! She'd put the fliers under the windshield wipers on all the parked cars. That way, everyone would get one, and she wouldn't have to hand them out in person.

She began holding the fliers and walking up and down the rows, carefully lifting the wipers as she slipped the papers underneath.

She was pleased with herself for coming up with such a good solution. She'd probably reach more people with this method anyway. Gregg would be proud of her.

When Laurie was through distributing the fliers, she realized she was stuck at school without a ride home. She had missed her bus, and it was too far to walk. Swinging her oversize canvas book bag over her shoulder, she headed for the pay phone inside the school to call Liz. She hoped her sister would be home. As she walked back through the parking lot, she found herself enjoying the crisp fall afternoon. It gave her a good feeling to know that she had done her job well, and it had proven to be pretty painless. She would also prove to Gregg that she was just as capable of helping him with his campaign as Nicole. She could hardly wait to see him at school the next day.

Chapter Five

Laurie sensed that something was wrong the moment she approached the lunch table. Her bright smile vanished as six pairs of eyes stared up at her.

"What's wrong?" she asked, setting down her lunch tray. She sat down quickly so that nobody would notice how much her knees were trembling.

"What's wrong is that you really messed up," said Nicole, shaking her head and acting thoroughly disgusted.

"What did I do?" asked Laurie as Gregg silenced Nicole with a dirty look.

"You didn't do anything wrong on purpose," explained Gregg. "It's just that you didn't give out the fliers the way you should have." His voice was gentle, but Laurie could read the disappointment in his dark eyes.

"What do you mean?" asked Laurie, feeling as though she were drowning in a sea of accusations. "I gave out every one of those fliers yesterday," she insisted.

"That's not true," cried Nicole, pointing her finger at Laurie. "You didn't give them out to anyone. You took the easy way out and stuck them under people's windshield wipers. *And* you managed to break the wipers on Eric Carlisle's brand-new car," she added, her lips pursed tightly together.

"Oh, *no!*" exclaimed Laurie, clapping her hand over her mouth. "I don't know how that could possibly have happened," she said. "I thought I was being so careful. I just wanted to make sure that everyone got one of the fliers. I wasn't having very much luck handing them out," she finished lamely.

"I'll bet you didn't even try to hand them out yourself," said Nicole, her aqua eyes narrowing as she stared across the table at Laurie.

"All right, Nicole. Just cool it. Laurie didn't break Eric's windshield wipers on purpose. It was an accident. But that wasn't really the best way to distribute fliers, Laurie. Most people throw away the advertisements they find on their windshields without even reading them. If you hand one to them personally, they'll usually at least take a look at it," Gregg said. "Did Nicole show you how to give them out?" he asked gently.

Laurie nodded, forced to admit the truth. "She did, but I didn't know any of the kids, and nobody paid any attention to me or the fliers," she said, her voice breaking. She tried to hold back the flood of tears that was threatening to spill from her eyes. Whatever happened, she wouldn't let herself cry in front of everyone. If she did, she'd be humiliated, and Nicole would be delighted.

Gregg reached for her hand. "Don't worry about it, Laurie. I guess it was a bad move on my part, asking you to hand out fliers. There are plenty of other things you'd be great at," he added reassuringly. "In the meantime, I'll talk to Eric and tell him what happened. I'm sure we can work something out."

Gregg's sympathetic attitude just made Laurie feel worse, and she had to bite her lip to keep it from trembling. She wished Gregg wouldn't make such a big deal about finding out how she could make a place for herself at New Brunswick High. She had hoped that she belonged with him, but he didn't seem to share her feelings.

"Tell Eric that I'll pay to have his wipers fixed. After all, it was my fault," she said, struggling to keep her voice steady.

Gregg nodded. "OK, but what's important is that you don't quit trying to find something to get involved in."

Laurie leaned forward so that only Gregg could hear her. Nicole was deep in conversation with Amy and Heather about a sale at the mall. "Maybe I should wait awhile before I get into activities here, Gregg," she said. "It always used to seem enough that we were friends. Unless you don't want to be anymore," she added miserably. The words had been difficult for her to get out but she desperately needed to know how he felt about her right then.

"Of course we're still friends, Laurie. But I can't be your only friend here," Gregg said, looking a bit annoyed. "Even in Skylar, we both had other friends, and that was a long time ago. Now we're older, and it's nice to have lots of friends and become involved in things. You can't keep thinking about the past, you know. It doesn't exist anymore. You'll miss out on too many great things right now."

Laurie didn't care about all the great things that were going on in New Brunswick. She *liked* to think about the past. It was warm and comfortable and full of wonderful memories. Now she was afraid that Gregg was slipping away from her, and she wasn't sure that she could transform herself into the kind of person he wanted her to be.

"Listen, Laurie, I've got a great idea," he said, slapping the tabletop with the palm of his hand. "The school play this year is *The Red Carnation*, and I've got one of the leads. You worked on the scenery for the play that we did in Skylar a couple of years ago, remember?"

Laurie nodded. It hadn't been much of a job, just painting backdrops and stage scenery, but she had enjoyed it—especially since Gregg had been in the school play that year as well.

"Well, why don't you come to our rehearsal after school today?" he suggested. "I'm sure the crew would love to have an extra pair of hands to help out, and I'll give you a great recommendation."

Laurie didn't know what to say. Gregg had no idea how difficult the move to Connecticut was turning out to be for her. Meeting new people and forming friendships seemed to come as easily to him as breathing, and he couldn't understand why it wasn't simple for her, too.

"OK, I'll give it a try," Laurie promised. She would have even considered tap dancing on top of the table if Gregg had asked her.

"That's terrific," said Gregg, squeezing her hand tightly. "Be prepared to go home all covered with green paint," he added. "They've been working on the flats for the park scene."

Laurie managed to relax somewhat. After all, what could possibly go wrong? The people on the stage crew were probably a great group of kids. And, anyway, how many kids at New Brunswick High could be as nasty as Nicole?

The school halls were silent when Laurie finally could stall no longer and pulled open the heavy doors to the auditorium. The lights in the seating area were dim, but the stage was brightly lit. Laurie hesitated for a moment before sitting down to watch the rehearsal. She had read *The Red Carnation* in

English class the year before. It was a one-act comedy about a middle-aged man and a young man who both supposedly met a pretty girl at a costume dance and asked her out on a date. None of the characters knew what the others looked like since they had only seen one another in costume. The girl agreed to meet each man separately at a park, telling them both to wear a red carnation so she'd recognize them. The two men met first and became very jealous of each other. When the girl finally arrived, the young man was so annoyed that he was ready to leave. The girl then admitted that the older man was really her father, who had wanted to check out the young man his daughter was meeting.

It was a cute play, and Laurie had enjoyed reading it at her old school. She watched for a while. Gregg was onstage, playing the part of the handsome young man. *Good casting,* she thought. Another boy was playing the father, and a very pretty brunette was standing between them. The auditorium was silent as Gregg spoke his lines, his brow furrowed in anger and his fists clenched at his sides. "I quit, I'm through!" he shouted. "I've been wasting my time with a pair of lunatics.

Goodbye Mr. Smith—*and* Miss Smith!" He walked quickly offstage.

"Good job, Gregg," a man called from the front row. Laurie assumed that he was the director. "Let's take a five-minute break to discuss your cues," he said, motioning for the trio of actors to join him offstage.

Laurie rose from her seat and walked the rest of the way down the aisle. When she reached the stage, she climbed the steps and walked backstage to a far corner. The painting crew was surrounded by cans of paint, brushes, and rollers strewn about in disarray. Everyone seemed to be laughing and joking as they worked on the flats that would form the city park backdrop.

The backdrop had grass, trees, flowers, and even birds. Two girls were busily painting a beautiful spring sky dotted with gentle clouds. Laurie found herself smiling. Gregg was right. She did need to make more of an effort to join things. Everyone looked so friendly that she was sure she'd have a great time working with the stage crew. And what was more, she'd get to see Gregg a lot, too.

Laurie stepped forward, looking around for the person in charge. She was just about to make her presence known when her heart suddenly seemed to stop beating. There, kneeling in a pair of designer jeans, her blond hair pulled back in a thick ponytail with a bright red ribbon, was Nicole. She was busy painting a patch of yellow and orange tulips and hadn't noticed Laurie at all.

Laurie took a step backward, almost tripping over a can of blue paint. She could never work on the stage crew with Nicole. It would be impossible. Nicole made her feel like a total idiot in every way. Even dressed to work on sets, the girl managed to look like a model who had just stepped off the page of some glamorous fashion magazine. Laurie felt about as glamorous as one of the people holding a wrench in *Popular Mechanics*. She knew she'd never be able to paint a single blade of grass as long as Nicole was around.

Laurie turned around and fled down the stage steps and out of the school building before anyone even noticed she had been there. If Gregg had seen her, he'd never have let her leave. As it was, she didn't know how she was going to explain anything to him. He liked Nicole, and it was very obvious that she more than liked him. Laurie wondered just what the status of their relationship really was. His whole group seemed to do things together, and so she wasn't sure whether or not Nicole and Gregg were a couple. One thing she was sure of, though, was that Nicole wanted them to be. Laurie could feel Nicole's resentment toward her whenever they were together. But Gregg didn't seem to realize that Nicole didn't like her, and Laurie was going to have a hard time explaining why she wasn't working on the play.

As Laurie reached the parking lot, she realized that once again she had missed the school bus and was without a ride home. She'd have to call a taxi since she knew both her mother and Liz were out. With a sigh she began the six-block walk to the nearest pay phone, to avoid a run-in with Gregg or Nicole. It was worth the extra effort.

Laurie stared out the taxi window, too exhausted after her difficult day to make small talk with the friendly driver. He asked her how long she had been living in New Brunswick, where she had lived before, and how she liked her new home so far. Laurie lied in answer to his last question, telling him that she loved it. The truth was that she was beginning to wish her family had never moved to New Brunswick at all. For over a year she had fantasized about being with Gregg again, but her dreams had been nothing like this. She had thought that she and Gregg would become more than just friends. She should have realized that they could never really become boyfriend and girlfriend.

Liz tried to tell me that, Laurie thought miserably. *But I wouldn't listen.* And now Gregg was trying to tell her the same thing. Nothing was working out at all.

Laurie paid the driver, counting the change into his hand, and then climbed out of the car. Her mom's station wagon was parked in the driveway. She must have gotten back early from her shopping trip, Laurie thought as she walked slowly up the brick path to their front door.

The house smelled like lemon furniture polish and window cleaner. "Mom? Where are you?" called Laurie, dropping her books on the hall table and heading toward the bright yellow kitchen.

"Hi, honey. How was your day?" asked Mrs. Raymond. She was sitting on a high wooden stool, cutting broccoli into a large glass bowl.

Laurie shrugged. "OK, I guess. I'm kind of tired, Mom, so I think I'll go up to my room until dinner's ready." She needed time to organize her thoughts so she'd know what to say to Gregg at school the next day. Not being able to hand out the fliers was one thing, but he'd never understand why she hadn't joined the scenery committee.

"That's fine, Laurie. Dinner will be at six-thirty. I've got a little surprise for you," said her mother.

"It's not such a little surprise," said Liz, coming in from the dining room with a handful of silverware. "The Crawfords are coming for dinner tonight."

"Oh, no!" cried Laurie, dropping onto a kitchen chair. "I can't see Gregg tonight."

"Why on earth not?" asked Mrs. Raymond. She stared at her daughter. "It's just an ordinary Tuesday evening, and we didn't have anything special planned. I thought you'd be thrilled by the news."

"Mom, you just don't understand," said Laurie, leaning her elbows on the table and resting her chin on her hands.

"I guess I don't. Why don't you try explaining," said her mother.

Laurie shook her head. "It's too involved. I'm going to my room for a while," she said, walking out of the kitchen. She felt doomed as she went up the stairs. She had thought

70

that she'd have until the next morning to tell Gregg about the play. Now she'd have to deal with it that night. Drained of all her energy, Laurie lay across her bed and drifted off to sleep.

"Laurie, the Crawfords are here," hissed Liz, tugging frantically at Laurie's arm.

Laurie sat up with a start and gasped as she looked at the little white alarm clock on her bedside table. Six forty-five! *How could it have gotten so late?* she thought in a panic.

"Mom wants you downstairs on the double," said Liz, closing the door behind her.

Laurie jumped up and hurried to her dressing table. The clothes she had worn to school were wrinkled, and her hair was a tangled mess. She pulled off her skirt and sweater, reaching for the nearest clean clothes, a pair of jeans and a faded denim work shirt. She rolled the shirt sleeves back to her elbows and turned up the collar, wishing once more that she had a flair for dressing, as Nicole did. After running a brush through her hair, she smoothed some peach-colored gloss on her lips and then stepped back to survey the results in the mirror. *Not great,* she decided, *but definitely better than I looked fif-*

71

teen minutes ago. It was the best she could do in such a short time. Taking a deep breath, she opened her bedroom door and went down to join the group.

Everyone was already seated in the dining room, and Gregg motioned for Laurie to take the empty chair next to his. "Hi," he said, greeting her with a grin. "This was a nice surprise, huh? I didn't find out we were coming for dinner tonight until I got home from rehearsal."

Laurie wished he wouldn't talk about the play at all. She smiled back weakly, then turned toward Gregg's parents to say hello.

Mrs. Crawford reached across the table to pat Laurie's hand. "It's so nice to see you again, dear," she said. "We were just talking about the last Christmas we all spent together."

Laurie felt relieved. Now there was something she'd feel comfortable discussing.

"I remember that," boomed Mr. Crawford. "You and Gregg picked out the tree for us, the biggest one we'd ever had."

"I strung popcorn for hours," said Laurie.

"And I tested the lights for hours," added Gregg. "It took me forever to find where that short was."

The dinner table conversation was pleasant, centering on the fond memories the two families shared. Laurie and Gregg talked about old friends and teachers, and Laurie kept hoping that everything would go that smoothly for the rest of the evening.

Then Gregg took a forkful of chocolate cake and said, "By the way, Laurie, I've been meaning to ask you how it went this afternoon. I didn't see you at rehearsal, but things were kind of hectic."

This is it, Laurie thought. "Um, I was going to join, Gregg," she began, groping. "But the more I thought about it, the more I decided that painting wasn't really for me. I'll find some other committee or club to join, though," she promised, looking down at the table-cloth to avoid his eyes.

"What are you talking about, Laurie?" he asked in surprise. "You seemed excited about it. You loved working on the stage sets for the play in Skylar."

"I'm sorry, Gregg," she said lamely. It would be impossible to explain her behavior without mentioning Nicole.

Gregg opened his mouth to speak and then, glancing around the table, seemed to change his mind. "Why don't we go and talk in the family room?" he suggested, pushing his chair away from the table.

Laurie nodded, feeling as though she had been summoned to the principal's office. As she followed Gregg, her parents, Liz, and the Crawfords cheerfully headed toward the living room.

Gregg sat down on the overstuffed corduroy couch and motioned for Laurie to join him. She remembered the countless times they had sat together on that very same sofa, but she couldn't remember ever feeling unhappy about it.

Gregg cleared his throat. "Why are you acting this way, Laurie?" he asked, sounding confused. "You used to do lots of things in Skylar—pep club, stage crew, the yearbook. What's so different here?"

Laurie shook her head, finding it difficult to explain her jumbled feelings. "You're expecting too much of me too soon, Gregg," she said, struggling to keep her voice even. "I'm not like you. I can't just leap into an enormous school and make a whole bunch of new friends."

"But you were never this shy or afraid of new things in Skylar," Gregg replied. "What's the difference if New Brunswick High is bigger? That means it has a lot more to offer. And you would have loved being on the scenery committee," he insisted.

"I'm sorry," she said softly. "It's just different. I wish you could understand how I feel." Laurie felt a nudge of resentment towards Gregg's stubbornness. She had been depending on him to be there for her. But maybe he had changed too much for that to be possible.

Chapter Six

"Mademoiselle Raymond, is it too much to ask that you attend my class in mind as well as in body?"

Laurie snapped her head up with a start and found herself staring at a row of neat white buttons that marched up to a well-starched collar. Her eyes traveled a bit farther, and she found herself face-to-face with a very annoyed Monsieur Jabon.

"I-I'm sorry," she stammered, her cheeks burning with embarrassment. As much as she hated to admit it, her teacher had a right to be angry with her this time. Instead of concentrating on the lesson, her mind had strayed. Just then, everything was much too complicated for her to handle. Gregg had been angry with her when he had left her house the night before, and she knew that his friends didn't really consider her one of their group. Laurie was beginning to think that she and Gregg might not even be able to be friends again, much less boyfriend and girlfriend.

"Well, since you've finally decided to join us, Mademoiselle Raymond, perhaps you would be so kind as to translate the following sentence into French," Monsieur Jabon continued unmercifully.

Laurie nodded, hoping she'd be able to handle the translation without drawing even more attention to herself. If she had been caught daydreaming in math or English, she might have had a fighting chance. But French was always a disaster, even when she *was* paying attention.

"Very well, then. For this lesson we were ordering a French meal, as if we were in a restaurant on the Champs-Élysées. Mademoiselle Lawson has ordered the appetizer, Monsieur Parker ordered the beverage, and now you shall order the entrée. Please translate this sentence: "We'll have some fish to start off."

Laurie took a deep breath and turned in her seat to face the class.

"*Oh, non, Mademoiselle,* please stand so we can all hear you," instructed Monsieur Jabon, his mustache twitching.

Laurie stood and swallowed, her fists clenched at her sides. If only she could remember the French word for fish.

"We'll have some fish . . ." prompted the teacher.

"*Nous allons prendre du poison pour commencer.*" Laurie let out the breath she had been holding and sank back gratefully into her seat. She was totally unprepared for the laughter that erupted in the classroom. Only Monsieur Jabon looked unamused. She couldn't imagine what she had done wrong and wished that she could vanish into thin air, or at least run out of the room. But Monsieur Jabon kept her riveted to her seat with his hostile glare.

"Perhaps you should spend more time studying and less time dreaming," he said tartly. He picked up a small piece of white chalk and scratched out two words on the blackboard: *poison* and *poisson*. "You ordered some poison to start your meal," he continued, pointing to the first word. "The French word for fish is *poisson*," he added disdainfully. "And it is pronounced with a hissing sound. *Poison* is poison, and is pronounced with a harder sound, more like an English *z*."

Laurie nodded. The class was still snickering and glancing in her direction. She was so anxious to leave the room that she almost tripped over her bag when the bell rang. That would have been the perfect grand finale, she thought dismally, heading toward the cafeteria.

Laurie had done her best to avoid Gregg for the past few days, and lately she had been spending her lunch periods in the library. He had called twice, but she had instructed Liz to say she wasn't home. She was just too embarrassed to speak to him. Without telling Gregg about Nicole, she couldn't give him a good reason for backing out of the scenery committee. Since he seemed to be on such close terms with Nicole, he'd never understand why Laurie couldn't work with her.

That day, however, Laurie wanted to see Gregg again. She needed some of his strength now. After being so humiliated in her French class, she couldn't bring herself to go to the library and sit by herself for forty-five minutes. She hoped he would tell her that everything would be all right and that she'd eventually fit in. At that point she wasn't sure that she ever would.

The cafeteria was crowded, as usual, and everyone was jockeying for a place in line. Ever since Nicole's comment about her childish brown bag, Laurie had been buying her lunch. Now she took a still-damp orange tray from the stack and pushed it along the chrome bars, choosing a cellophane-wrapped tuna sandwich and a cup of vegetable soup. She wasn't really that hungry, but if she didn't have a full tray, Nicole would undoubtedly make some sarcastic remark again.

When she reached the register, she looked up to see if Gregg was at his usual table. Sure enough, he was there with the rest of the crowd. Nicole was giggling as she cupped her hand under a forkful of spaghetti and tried to feed it to Gregg, who was sitting beside her. At first he resisted, leaning back in his seat, but he finally gave in and ate the spaghetti, laughing along with the triumphant Nicole.

Feeling hot tears of frustration burning her eyes, Laurie knew she couldn't join the group.

How could she cope with having to watch Gregg and Nicole together like that? She finally carried her tray to the opposite corner of the cafeteria, taking a vacant chair next to a girl who was so deeply immersed in a textbook that she didn't even bother to look up.

That's what I might as well be doing, thought Laurie sadly. She forced herself to take a bite of her sandwich and then pushed the tray away. The huge lump in her throat made it impossible to eat. Somehow she'd have to see Gregg alone—that is, if there was anyplace where Nicole wouldn't be able to intrude. They needed to have a long, private talk.

"There is only one way to settle it. She must choose between us." Laurie, watching in the darkened auditorium, thought that Gregg read his line beautifully.

"We might flip coins to see which one of us stays," said the other boy in the play.

Gregg shook his head. "No, I refuse to treat the matter in such a trivial way. If I leave, it will be at the request of the lady." He folded his arms across his chest, standing with his legs planted firmly apart in a picture of defiance.

"OK, gang, that's it for today," called the director. He rose from his seat in the first row. "You all were great, but let's see if you can memorize some more lines so that you can throw away your scripts. See you Monday afternoon—and have a great weekend," he added, slipping into his jacket and heading out the side door of the auditorium.

Laurie, who had been standing in the rear of the auditorium, still wasn't sure how to approach Gregg. Thankfully, Nicole was nowhere in sight, but Gregg was zipping up his jacket. In another couple of minutes he would be gone, and so would her opportunity to speak to him.

"Gregg," she called, hurrying down the aisle toward him.

His dark eyes widened in surprise. "Hi, Laurie," he said, picking up his stack of books. "What brings you here?"

Laurie shook her head. "I just wanted to talk to you," she said hesitantly.

He nodded. "Funny, I wouldn't have thought so by the way you've been avoiding me lately. I tried to call you a couple of times, and I haven't even seen you in the cafeteria for the past few days," he said.

Laurie was startled. She had thought that

Gregg was angry with her and that he didn't want to see her at all. Liz had been right when she had told Laurie to take his calls. "I haven't been avoiding you, Gregg," she said. "I *was* in the cafeteria today, but you looked kind of busy," she added, trying to erase any trace of jealousy from her voice. The last thing she wanted to do was make him angry again.

"How could I have been busy? I was only eating lunch," he protested, shrugging. "Why didn't you just come over and say hello? Everyone wondered where you were."

Laurie found it hard to believe that she'd actually been missed. Nicole certainly hadn't been anxious about her. "Sorry, I guess I should have," she replied lamely. "I had a lot of studying to do, so I sat by myself."

"You really spend too much time by yourself," said Gregg. "You need to get involved with other people—besides me," he added pointedly.

Laurie froze. Did he mean that he didn't even want to be friends anymore?

"Listen, Laurie," he continued, taking a seat and motioning for her to sit beside him, "I know how tough it is to start at a new school, and I did it myself not too long ago. The kids here are great, they really are. If you'd only give them a chance—"

"Gregg, I'm not you, OK? I don't have the same talent for getting along with people. I try, I really do, but you've always been my best friend," she blurted out and then bit her lip as she realized what she had said. Her feelings were so jumbled that they had just spilled out on their own.

"Oh, Gregg, everything used to be so simple. I wish that I had some kind of magical time machine, and we could go back to Skylar," she said with a huge sigh.

"I wouldn't want to go back," said Gregg firmly. "I'm happy in New Brunswick, and you will be too once you make some new friends here. You think about the past too much, Laurie. Let it go," he urged.

Suddenly his seriousness vanished, and he smiled warmly. "Listen, Nicole's throwing this huge campaign party for me at her house tomorrow night. I'd really like you to go with me," he said, his fingers curling warmly about her own.

Laurie's skin tingled at his touch. There was nothing she wanted more than to be with Gregg, but the thought of being at Nicole's house put a damper on things. Yet how could she turn him down after that big speech he'd just given her about meeting new people and getting involved at school? "I'd really like to go with you, Gregg," she replied with a shaky smile.

"Great. Just dress casually, and I'll pick you up at seven-thirty," he said, jumping to his feet and waiting for her to follow him out of the auditorium. "How about a ride home? I might even be persuaded to stop and buy you a chocolate-chocolate-chip ice-cream cone," he said, teasing her.

Laurie grinned, pleased that Gregg still remembered her favorite flavor of ice cream. "You've got a deal," she said happily as they headed toward the parking lot.

"What does 'dress casually' mean?" asked Laurie, her gray eyes worried. She had already gone through her entire closet, and she still had no idea what to wear.

"What do you think it means?" replied Liz, reaching out to give her sister a gentle shake. "It means dress casually. Forget the evening gown and leave off the sequins," she teased.

Laurie turned to face her sister. "I know Gregg wants me to fit in with his friends, and I've really been trying hard," she said.

"But it doesn't seem to be working so far. I want to be dressed like all the rest of the girls at Nicole's."

"Well, what about your blue wool skirt with the matching vest? You can even borrow my white silk blouse," offered Liz.

Laurie shook her head. "That sounds as if I'm going to a job interview, not to a party."

"Then how about a real nice pair of designer jeans and a pretty sweater?" suggested Liz, still trying to be helpful.

"Nope," vetoed Laurie. "That's *too* casual."

Liz threw her hands up in the air. "I give up," she said in despair. "I feel like all we've been doing lately is trying to choose clothes for you, and it's getting out of hand. You decide what to wear, but don't blame me if Nicole is wearing a pink and white tutu, and you aren't dressed the same way," she said, turning toward the door.

"No!" cried Laurie in a panic. "I'm really sorry, Liz," she apologized. "I don't mean to be such a pain. It's just that I haven't had much luck making new friends yet, and I'm not even sure how much of a friend Gregg is anymore," she finished softly.

Liz came back into the bedroom and sat down on Laurie's white antique desk chair.

"I'm sure that Gregg still cares about you, Laurie," she said reassuringly. "It's just that he wants you to have other interests, too."

Laurie shook her head. "It's hopeless," she said, sounding so forlorn that Liz jumped up and began pulling all of Laurie's dresser drawers open.

"Now look here, kiddo, we're not going to quit until we've gone through every single piece of clothing you own. Eventually we'll find the perfect outfit, just the way we did for your last date."

Laurie couldn't help smiling at her sister's surge of enthusiasm. "OK, if you say so," she agreed, watching as Liz held up one sweater after another, discarding some and putting a few possibilities aside in a pile. Suddenly she paused.

"How about your beige corduroys and my cashmere pullover?" Liz suggested.

Laurie thought for a moment. "You know, that might work," she agreed.

"I'll be back in a second with the sweater," promised Liz, dashing out of the room.

By the time Gregg arrived an hour later, Laurie had changed three more times and fixed her hair at least half a dozen ways. She'd finally settled on the beige cords and sweater combination that Liz had suggested, and she left her hair to fall gently below her shoulders the way she usually wore it.

Gregg's only comment was his usual, "You look great, Laurie." But as she sat in the front seat of his car listening to one of her favorite songs on the radio, she wondered if his compliment had been sincere, or if he was just being polite.

There was no doubt that *he* looked great. Gregg's wavy dark brown hair curled slightly around his ears, and the black sweater and jeans he was wearing showed off his muscular build. Laurie was sure that every girl at the party would find Gregg gorgeous. She certainly did.

"Remember how you used to love old sixties' songs?" she asked him as they headed north toward Nicole's neighborhood.

Gregg laughed. "What do you mean, used to?" he asked, opening the glove compartment and pulling out a stack of tapes. "Here, pick one."

Laurie was amazed at the large selection. "It's hard to choose," she said, glancing at all the familiar titles.

"How about the Beach Boys?" asked Gregg, popping a tape into the deck. He nodded his head in time to the beat of the music, and soon both he and Laurie were singing along.

Laurie relaxed. It was so much fun, just the way it used to be between them. Laurie was glad she had come, and she felt sure that they could recapture the relationship they had once had. All they needed was more time alone together like this. But her happiness soon turned to apprehension as Gregg swung the car down the circular drive to Nicole's Tudor-style house. The driveway and road were already crowded with cars, but Gregg managed to maneuver his car between two others.

"Let's go," he said, pocketing the keys and giving Laurie's hand a squeeze. "We're going to have a terrific time."

Laurie wished she could hold Gregg to that promise. She *had* been having a great time until just then, but she had a feeling things would change very fast.

"This is a beautiful house," she said, trying to sound positive.

"It sure is," agreed Gregg. "Nicole's father is president of some fashion company. It's really nice of her to hold the campaign party here." He rang the bell confidently, and the door was answered by a uniformed maid. Once their coats had been taken, Gregg led Laurie into a huge living room that was overflowing with kids. Gregg knew just about everyone there, and most everyone came over to say hello.

A maid offered Laurie and Gregg soft drinks. Nicole sidled up to Gregg. "I hope you're enjoying the party," she said, looking concerned. "I planned it all just for you." Once again she had managed to look like a fashion model, in blue and green cotton pants and an oversize aqua sweater that matched her eyes perfectly.

"It's great, Nicole, just great," Gregg replied. "I don't know how to thank you. Isn't this a terrific party, Laurie?" he added, trying to include her in the conversation.

Laurie nodded, caught off guard, and almost spilled her soda all over Liz's cashmere sweater and Nicole's thick white carpeting. "It is, Nicole, and you've thought of everything," she said, trying to sound as friendly as she could.

Nicole barely glanced her way, keeping her attention riveted on Gregg. "Could I borrow you for a few minutes, Gregg?" she asked. "We're setting up a small stage for you downstairs in the family room, and I want to make

91

sure that you like where the men are putting it."

"Sure," said Gregg, turning toward Laurie. "Will you be OK by yourself?" he asked, hesitating.

Laurie smiled brightly. "Of course," she said, hoping her words sounded convincing.

"I'll be back in a few minutes," promised Gregg, letting himself be led away by Nicole. "Try to meet some people," he whispered over his shoulder.

"That's easy for *you* to say," Laurie mumbled to herself, as she looked around the crowded room. In the marble-floored hallway, some kids were dancing, and others were sampling delicate sandwiches in the dining room. She forced herself to leave the safety of the corner where she had been hiding and ventured into the beautifully decorated dining room.

The crystal chandelier, which threw off diamond pinpoints of light, was the focal point of the room. Laurie had never been in such an elegant house before, and it made her feel even more intimidated by Nicole. She had guessed that her family was well-off, but . . . She looked around for a familiar face and saw Heather and Amy deeply involved in a conversation with a third girl, whom Laurie had never seen before. *This is the perfect opportunity to meet people,* Laurie reminded herself, heading toward the trio.

"Hi," she said with a friendly smile. "Great party, isn't it?"

The three girls stopped talking for a moment to glance at Laurie. "Nicole always throws great parties," said Heather flatly.

"Are you guys going to Josie's party next week?" asked Amy, directing her question toward her two friends.

"If Steve asks me," said the girl Laurie didn't know. Apparently no one was going to introduce them.

As the conversation continued around her, Laurie moved on. She felt uncomfortable standing there while the girls discussed things that didn't involve her.

Her eyes roamed the crowded room. The girl she had sat next to on the bus a few days before was helping herself to a miniature pastry. Laurie hurried to join her. "Do they taste as good as they look?" she asked, trying to make conversation.

"Uh, yeah. Sure," said the girl with a brief smile. "Are you a friend of Nicole's?" she asked.

"I'm more a friend of Gregg's," answered Laurie truthfully.

"He's a great guy," said the girl. "And he'll make a terrific class president."

As Laurie started to reply, she saw that the girl's attention had been caught by someone across the room.

"That's my boyfriend," explained the girl, nodding toward a tall blond boy who was staring in their direction. "I'll see you later," she said, as she moved away.

Laurie nodded understandingly. "Sure," she said, retreating against the wall. *This isn't working at all*, she thought. Maybe she was trying too hard, but she didn't know any other way to go about making new friends. She'd be lucky if she made even one. Everybody at New Brunswick High seemed to be part of a select clique, and it was hard for someone new to break in.

"Everyone downstairs to the family room," called a familiar voice, and Laurie turned to see Nicole waving from the doorway. "Gregg's going to make his speech," she said enthusiastically.

Jason, who had just arrived, led the group in a cheer as they headed downstairs, with Laurie at the end of the line. Gregg was standing on a makeshift stage at the end of the huge room. He waved his hands to quiet everyone and then began to speak. His sincerity came through loud and clear, and it was easy for Laurie to see why he hadn't had any trouble making friends in Connecticut. His warm, outgoing manner said, "Hey, I'm on your side."

Laurie felt a rush of pride and sadness as she listened. She couldn't hope to hold on to Gregg for herself any longer. He was a very special person, and everyone wanted a piece of him for themselves. He had moved ahead with his life, and now Laurie would have to do the same—before she lost him for good. The only trouble was, she didn't know where to start.

Chapter Seven

"After your party, Nicole, Monday morning seems even duller than usual," complained Amy with a sigh.

"It was a dynamite party," agreed Heather, smiling at Nicole, who was enjoying all the lavish compliments.

"Absolutely," said Jason. "And after Crawford's speech, I don't think there's any doubt about who our next class president will be."

Nicole nodded in agreement. "That's true, Gregg. Everyone loved your speech. Ken Roberts doesn't stand a chance running against you," she added, her blue eyes shining with admiration.

Gregg shook off their praise. "Don't you believe it. Ken is a good speaker, too. You can't knock him out of the election," he said firmly. He turned suddenly toward Laurie. "You're awfully quiet."

She was startled by the unexpected attention, and the truth was that she had purposely avoided joining in their discussion of the party. She couldn't agree with everyone about how wonderful it had been since she had had such a miserable time. "I was listening," she replied, forcing a smile. But she sensed that Gregg wasn't fooled. He knew her too well for that.

"But you've hardly touched your lunch," he protested, nodding toward the slice of cold pizza that seemed permanently stuck to the paper plate.

Laurie shrugged. "I'm too tired to eat. I was up pretty late last night studying for French. Monsieur Jabon and I aren't exactly best buddies."

"Oh, that's no problem," said Heather with a toss of her head. Her bright yellow feather earrings shook merrily. "I had to repeat his class, and then I finally decided to fulfill my language requirement by taking Spanish."

"You're kidding," said Laurie, shocked. If there was one thing she didn't want to do, it was to go through an additional semester of French with such a difficult teacher.

"Don't worry about it," advised Gregg, waving Heather's comments aside. "I had Jabon, too, and as long as you study, you'll do OK in his class. He's not going to win any popularity contests, but he does respect the kids who are really trying." Gregg rose from the table as the bell rang. "I've got a history exam this period, and I need to check a couple of dates with one of the kids in my class," he said, picking up his thick history textbook. "I'll see you guys later," he called over his shoulder.

Laurie watched him go, feeling an emptiness settle in over the table. Without Gregg, there was no reason for her to stay, so she packed up her books as well. Forcing a smile, she waved goodbye to the group, but nobody seemed to notice her departure. They were all engrossed in conversation about the upcoming election, which seemed to be their main topic of conversation lately.

The corridors were crowded, and by the

time Laurie reached her English class, she remembered that her class was meeting in the library that day. *Now I'll be late for sure*, she thought, glancing at her watch. Laurie turned and half ran down the long hallway, and she was completely out of breath by the time she swung open the glass doors and burst into the library.

"Sorry I'm late," she whispered as Mrs. McDonald waved her over to a table toward the rear of the room. "I forgot we were meeting in the library today."

The young teacher smiled. "That's all right, Laurie. We're doing some biographical research on William Shakespeare today. Why don't you see if there are still any books about him on the shelves?" she said, pointing toward the stacks.

Laurie nodded and headed off in that direction. Seeing friendly Mrs. McDonald always put her in a good mood, especially after a bad class with Monsieur Jabon. Laurie briefly wondered how two such entirely different people could end up in the same profession. Shrugging to herself as she set about finding a book, she decided not to think about Monsieur Jabon right then.

"But I don't think he really likes her at all.

He just feels sorry for her." The girl's high-pitched whisper sounded familiar to Laurie, and she recognized the voice as Nicole's. She hesitated before turning the corner.

"I know. I feel so sorry for Gregg," agreed a softer voice, which Laurie thought was Heather's. "She can't seem to do anything without him."

"Did you notice how he's always telling her to get involved in things, but she never does? Maybe she can't do anything on her own," said Nicole, and the two girls dissolved in giggles.

Laurie backed up quickly, as if she had been bitten by a poisonous snake. She knew that the girls weren't exactly her friends, but she hadn't known how much they disliked her until that moment. Was that how she came across to everyone, as the girl from Gregg's past who was dragging him down?

She quickly pulled a book from the shelf and spent the rest of the period huddled over it, but she wasn't able to think about anything except the conversation she had just overheard. Her chest felt as if it were ready to explode with hurt and anger. How could Gregg's friends talk about her behind her back like that? And how dare they describe her as some kind of loser! There were plenty of things that she knew how to do.

For one thing, she could join a choral group. Everyone was always telling her what a good voice she had. She and Gregg had even performed a country-and-western duet in junior high. Or she could tutor other kids in English. She had always helped Gregg with his grammar and punctuation on assignments. But why did everything always have to come back to Gregg? She wondered if there might be any truth to Nicole's hurtful words. Maybe she *had* been relying on Gregg too much, expecting him to take care of her. Well, she'd just have to make her own way and forget about Gregg for now. One thing was sure; she was determined to show everyone how capable and independent she really was, even if it killed her. This time, she would choose her own projects and make her own friends. She had spent too much time and effort trying to relive the past with Gregg.

As the bell rang and the kids began to file out of the library, Laurie felt as if she were looking at New Brunswick High for the first time. She passed the huge cork bulletin board in the main hallway and realized that she had never paid any attention to its dozens of notices. Now a large, bright yellow poster caught her eye, and she smiled as she read the gold-faced words. The ad featured an adorable bloodhound dog with drooping brown eyes, his black nose pressed to the ground. Below him was printed, "If you've got a nose for news, the *New Brunswick News* needs you!"

This was the perfect opportunity for her, just exactly what she needed. She enjoyed writing, and she honestly felt that it was something she could do well. Why hadn't she thought of working on the school paper earlier? She must have been too engrossed in Gregg, trying out all his suggestions. From the time Laurie was a little girl, she had filled endless notebooks with her stories and poems, sharing a few with her family and Gregg, but keeping most of them private. She had even been a reporter on the school newspaper in Skylar, and their faculty adviser had told her that she had real talent. Now, if only she could convince the editor here—whoever he or she was—that she'd be an asset to the staff, she might be able to prove that Laurie Raymond was a lot more than Gregg Crawford's shadow.

*   *   *

The *New Brunswick News* office was on the second floor of the school building. Laurie's resolve faltered a bit as she approached Room 261 after school that day. She might not have entered if the door hadn't swung open at that exact moment, almost knocking her down.

"Oops, sorry," apologized a pretty brunette, her short hair flying in wisps about her face. She fixed her large, expressive brown eyes on Laurie. "Hi, I'm Robyn Jacobsen," she said cheerfully. "I'd like to say that I'm not usually in this much of a hurry, but the truth is that I am." The girl grinned, stepping aside to let Laurie enter.

"I'm Laurie Raymond. Weren't you on your way out?" she asked, as Robyn followed her into a large room filled with desks and staffers.

"Actually, I was on my way to interview Mr. Scott about the new video setup the school bought, but I just remembered that he was out sick today. It's going to be great, though," she said, bubbling over with enthusiasm. "Whenever a group of kids takes a field trip, they can film it and share it later with the rest of the school. The kids who want to go into film editing will get to use the equipment, too. It's this real small VHS camera and cassette player. Sorry," she said, looking sheepish. "I guess I get carried away when I'm excited about something. I never even asked why you were here." Robyn hoisted herself up onto a high wooden stool near a countertop overflowing with newspaper copy.

Laurie smiled. Robyn was one of the most outgoing people she had ever met. She felt her shyness melting away in the warmth that Robyn projected. "I saw a poster in the library," she began. "You know, the one with the bloodhound. I thought I'd see if there were still any openings for reporters."

It was exciting to be back in a newspaper office. She hadn't realized how much she missed working on the paper in Skylar, and the *New Brunswick News* was very popular with the students. It would be fun to accomplish something creative. Besides, Laurie had a feeling she'd enjoy working with Robyn. Maybe Robyn would even prove to be her first real friend here, one she'd made on her own. Laurie was beginning to understand that Gregg didn't have to choose her friends for her.

Robyn was smiling. "Isn't that a terrific poster?" she asked, her dark eyes twinkling. "Ron Marshall did it. He's a fantastic artist, and it's a picture of his own dog. Can you believe it?"

Laurie laughed. "He *is* good," she agreed.

"Anyway," said Robyn, playing with the long strand of beads that hung around her neck, "it just so happens that there *is* an opening for a reporter here. A good one, that is," she added, eyeing Laurie. "Have you ever worked on a school newspaper before?"

Laurie nodded. "I just moved here from up-state New York, and I was a reporter on our school paper there. It was pretty small, though. If you'd like, I could bring in a batch of articles I've written," she offered.

"Hey, that would be great," said Robyn, hopping down from her stool and reaching for a sheet of white notebook paper. "Steve Graham is our editor in chief, and he's the guy to see when you bring in your stuff. Is that OK?" she asked, looking up from the note she was scribbling.

"Sure," said Laurie. Everything was happening so quickly that she could hardly believe it. But this time she would be involved in a project *she* was interested in, not something Gregg had suggested. And best of all, Nicole wouldn't be anywhere in sight.

"OK, then be here tomorrow at lunchtime,"

instructed Robyn. "Almost everybody who works on the paper spends their lunch period here. There's always so much to do that we bring sandwiches from home and eat while we work. But it's kind of fun," she added quickly, turning her head to the side and studying Laurie. "I'd always planned on becoming a journalist," she continued with a friendly smile, "but even if I hadn't, it's great to work with the kids on the paper. There isn't one rotten apple in the bunch."

Laurie thought of Nicole once again.

"Sometimes we have to interview one of the New Brunswick snobs, as I call them, but we don't have to work with them every day. I'd hate that," said Robyn, wrinkling her nose. "Are you interested in writing as a career?" she asked, abruptly changing the subject.

Laurie paused. "I'm not really sure yet," she said. "But I've always loved to write. Poetry is my favorite," she added, surprised at how candidly she was confiding in a virtual stranger.

Robyn nodded understandingly. "I've always loved to write, too. Only not poetry. That's too hard for me. I do a lot of short stories, and I've even sent some of them in to magazines. But so far all I've gotten are rejection slips," she admitted.

"Isn't it an awful feeling to get your stuff back in the mail?" Laurie said. "I've sent some poems in to magazines, too, and I've gotten a lot of pink slips myself."

"Don't worry, Laurie. Someday we'll both be famous," said Robyn with certainty. "I have it all planned out."

"I wish I had your confidence," Laurie admitted.

"It'll rub off on you if we work together," promised Robyn, checking her watch. "I'm late again, as usual," she said, reaching for her brown suede jacket. "I've got tennis lessons two afternoons a week, and the poor instructor still hasn't gotten used to my being late all the time. Do you play tennis?" she asked, picking up her books and heading toward the door.

Laurie nodded. "A little. I never took lessons, though," she added. She and Gregg used to play tennis together in Skylar, but neither of them had any formal training.

"Maybe we could play together sometime," suggested Robyn, holding the door open for Laurie. "Do you need a ride home? The buses have already left."

"I'd love one," said Laurie gratefully. "But I live way over on Shady Brook Lane." She hoped she wouldn't be taking Robyn out of her way.

"That's perfect. My lesson is on Chestnut Hill, and that's only about a mile or so from Shady Brook. Do you drive?" she asked.

"Yes, but I don't have my own car," Laurie replied. "I guess I should think about getting one—if I'll be staying after school working on the paper, though."

"I'd be dead without mine," said Robyn as they reached the parking lot.

"My mom might let me borrow her car sometimes," said Laurie, thinking aloud. If she offered to run some errands for her mother after school, she was sure she'd be allowed to borrow the wagon.

"My mother used to let me borrow her car, but it was always such a hassle," said Robyn, shifting her car into gear. "I worked summers and afternoons after school until I had enough money to buy this old girl on my own. Well, to be honest," she admitted, "my dad helped me with a big chunk of money on my birthday. It was the best present I ever got. I even took a course in auto mechanics at the YMCA so that if anything goes wrong with the car, I won't be stuck on a road some-where waiting for a knight on a white horse to show up. You know what I mean?"

Laurie laughed. "I take it you're pretty independent," she said admiringly.

"Absolutely," said Robyn, pulling the little car onto Main Street. "I wouldn't have anything against being rescued by a tall, handsome stranger, but I don't want to have to count on it," she said.

"That makes a lot of sense," said Laurie, thinking of her strained relationship with Gregg.

"Of course it does," said Robyn. "I was thinking of doing an advice-to-the-lovelorn column for the *News*, but our beloved editor in chief decided against it. He said that people should mind their own business and not tell other people how to run their lives. He only believes in reporting straight, hard, cold facts," said Robyn, making her voice deep as she imitated Steve Graham.

Laurie laughed again. "I think you'd make a great advice columnist," she said. "I'll be your first case," she offered, only half joking.

"Uh-oh. Boy problems already? You just moved here!" said Robyn, turning to stare at Laurie as they stopped for a red light.

"I brought them along with me," said Laurie, amazed how comfortable she felt with Robyn.

"Let me get this straight, now. You brought along the boy, or the problems?" Robyn asked, sounding confused.

Laurie sighed. "Both," she answered. But for the first time she at least felt hopeful about her future at New Brunswick High. Maybe Gregg had been right. There *were* some great kids at school. It was just taking her a little while to find them.

Chapter Eight

All Tuesday morning Laurie kept glancing at her watch. She counted the hours and then the minutes until lunchtime, when she could race upstairs to Room 261 and submit her four best *Skylar Scoop* articles to Steve Graham. When the bell finally rang, the long corridors were even more crowded than usual. It seemed to take Laurie forever to reach the second-floor office.

It had been fun being with Robyn, and Laurie was anxious to see her again. But as she pushed open the wooden door to the converted classroom, she couldn't find the pretty brunette anywhere among the staffers who were all busy at work.

A tall, slender girl with long, thick blond hair in a single braid down her back looked up from one of the desks. "May I help you?" she asked, taking off her wire-rimmed glasses.

Laurie smiled nervously. She was still treading on new ground, and she wasn't sure how these kids would react to her. Robyn had been friendly enough, but that didn't mean that everyone on the newspaper staff would be. "I'm looking for Robyn Jacobsen," she said, her eyes scanning the room once more.

"Robyn had to go out on an interview," explained the girl with a pleasant smile. "Are you a friend of hers?"

"Sort of," Laurie said, smiling back. "I was applying for a job on the paper, and she told me to bring some sample articles in to Steve today."

"Oh, that's great. We could sure use some extra help around here. By the way, I'm Shelly. What's your name?" The girl reached for the manila envelope that Laurie was still clutching tightly in her hands.

"Laurie Raymond," she said, reluctantly handing over her work. "Is Steve around?"

she asked, wondering if she should see him personally or wait for Robyn to come back.

"I'm afraid that Steve's not here right now, either," said Shelly. "But I'm the assistant editor, so I'll make sure that he gets this," she promised, slipping the envelope into a small slot marked Editor.

Laurie nodded, not sure what to do next. She was dying to know if she'd get the job, but she didn't want to pressure Shelly. After all, she had just met the girl, and Steve had to read her articles before he could make a decision, anyway. She didn't know if she could wait that long without exploding. She had lain awake for hours the night before thinking about being a reporter for the *New Brunswick News*. At first she had only wanted it as a way to show Gregg and his friends how capable and talented she really was, but now she wanted to become involved for her own satisfaction as well. It would be fun finally working with people who shared her interests. She could hardly wait to receive her first assignment—if she got the job, that is.

"We'll be in touch with you soon," Shelly promised, turning back to the copy of the *News* that she had been reading.

Laurie backed toward the door. There was nothing to do now but wait it out. She nodded her thanks and headed into the hallway. She still had enough time to grab a sandwich in the cafeteria, but she wasn't ready to see Gregg or any of his crowd yet. She couldn't forget the conversation that she had overheard and the terrible hurt it had caused. Even if she didn't get the job on the paper, she was determined to show them that she wasn't just a wimp who needed to hold on to Gregg for support. She was perfectly capable of standing on her own two feet without help from anybody else. Deciding that she might as well spend this extra time with her French textbook, she turned toward the library. If Monsieur Jabon respected students who knew their stuff, then she had better begin proving herself to him as well. She had gotten off to a poor start at New Brunswick High, but she was determined to begin all over again. And this time she'd do it on her own.

All that evening Laurie waited anxiously for a phone call. This time she wasn't hoping to hear from Gregg, but from Robyn or Steve. She knew that the chances of anyone having read her articles and made a decision so soon were pretty slim. The call finally came the following evening, just as Laurie was about to step into the shower after supper.

She hurriedly pulled on her pink terry cloth robe and dove onto her bed, taking the light-weight plastic telephone along with her.

"Hold on, Laurie, because you've got the job!" shouted Robyn.

"Are you sure?" Laurie gasped.

"Of course I'm sure. Steve would have called you himself, but I asked him to let me do it," Robyn said with a giggle. "I love being the bearer of glad tidings. But honestly, Laurie, he just flipped over your articles. He even let me read them and they're really terrific."

Laurie felt as if she might explode with happiness. She really had gotten the job, and she'd done it all on her own.

"Aren't you going to say anything?" asked Robyn. "Like 'hallelujah,' or 'How much work will I have to do?'"

"I don't know what to say. This is all so unreal," Laurie began, trying to digest the news. "I mean, I really wanted to get the job, but I wasn't sure that I would." Robyn could never understand how much this opportunity meant to her.

"How could you have doubted it? You're a dynamite writer," said Robyn firmly. "And Steve already has a first assignment planned for you."

"You're kidding. What is it?" asked Laurie anxiously. *Maybe it's some glamorous interview*, she thought. *Anything, as long as I don't have to interview Nicole.*

"Do you think I'd take the fun out of all this suspense?" Robyn said, laughing. "Not on your life. Just show up at the newspaper office after school on Friday, and your assignment will be written out for you," she instructed. "I've got to run now. My mom has an aerobics class tonight, and I'm supposed to clean up after dinner. Anyway, I've got to go, but I'll see you Friday."

Laurie didn't replace the receiver right away. She felt absolutely wonderful. How would she ever last two whole days until Friday? She got off her bed and practically floated downstairs to talk to her mother.

Mrs. Raymond was in the living room, watching an old Bette Davis movie on TV. It must have been a real tearjerker, because she had a whole bunch of tissues wadded up beside her on the couch.

"Mom, could I speak with you for a minute?" Laurie asked.

"It's almost time for the commercial, honey," replied her mother, dabbing at her eyes. As the scene faded and a deodorant commercial flashed on, she turned to Laurie with a watery smile. "Bette Davis has gone blind, but she's so brave about it."

"It's only a movie, Mom. And I think you've seen it before, anyway," said Laurie. She didn't understand how her mother could get so worked up over old movies.

"Oh, I love these old pictures. You know that," said Mrs. Raymond, reaching for her daughter's hand. "Now, what did you want to talk to me about?" she asked.

"Well, it's just that I've been accepted for a job as a reporter on the school newspaper, and I'm going to need transportation home from school practically every day," she explained.

"Oh, Laurie, I'm so glad that you're finally getting involved at school. Gregg's mother says that he just loves New Brunswick High, and he's active in so many things there. She told me that he's even running for class president," she said.

Laurie nodded. "Yes, he is. And I'm really excited about this newspaper job, Mom, but I need a way to get home."

Mrs. Raymond smiled. "I take it you're making a plead for a car," she said, looking into Laurie's gray eyes.

"I guess I am," Laurie replied. "Most of the other kids here drive to school. I know I can't do it all the time, but could I borrow your car just a few days a week?" she asked hopefully.

Mrs. Raymond laughed, reaching out to touch Laurie's silky brown hair. "I think we might be able to work something out," she agreed. "With three cars in this family, we ought to be able to free one up for you when you need it." The commercial ended, and Mrs. Raymond turned back to her movie.

Laurie tiptoed away and climbed the stairs to her bedroom. She hadn't felt that happy in a long time, and she was proud of herself for taking the first important steps toward being on her own. She didn't even mind the awful forest-green carpeting her mother had promised to have replaced as soon as they had a free moment. One day her room would be perfect, with everything exactly the way she wanted it. *Just like my life*, Laurie thought.

One by one, things would begin to fall into place, starting with her new job on the school newspaper and her new friendship with Robyn. Then, if only she and Gregg would be able to work out their difficulties and have a real friendship, she wouldn't ask for anything more. She had already decided not to say anything yet to Gregg about working on the paper. She wanted to wait to tell him until she was sure she was off to a good start.

Laurie leaned forward to study her reflection in the dressing-table mirror. Running her fingers through her long, shiny brown hair, she wondered if maybe it was time to change her looks along with her personality. If she was going to be the new, confident Laurie Raymond, then she had better look the part. She pulled her hair to one side, clipping it with an oversize ivory barrette. She shook her head, wrinkling her nose in distaste. That wasn't much of a change. Then, she bent her head toward the floor, brushed her hair backward, and caught it in a knot on top of her head. But instead of making her look older and more sophisticated, the upswept style made her neck look scrawny and her ears stick out. Laurie let her long hair fall back to her shoulders again and went to search for her herbal shampoo and conditioner. She'd never be able to manage the transformation by herself, but maybe Robyn could help her. She had been wearing a terrific jumpsuit the day that Laurie had met her in the newspaper office, and she certainly knew how to apply makeup well.

Laurie stepped into the bathroom and adjusted the shower controls until the cascading water was so hot that the vanity mirror fogged up with steam. She hung her robe on the door hook and stepped under the strong spray. As she took a deep breath, feeling the water relax her tense muscles, her mind wandered back to the new image that she wanted to create for herself. She had to admit that she hoped the new Laurie would finally make Gregg interested in her as more than a friend again. She also wouldn't mind showing Nicole and her friends that they had misjudged Laurie Raymond. Of course, she didn't want to impose on Robyn too much, and changing her look might take quite a bit of work. The pretty brunette probably had lots of other friends at school, and Laurie didn't want to start clinging to her the way she had clung to Gregg.

Laurie closed her eyes and turned her face up to the water. Life was so complicated. One minute everything seemed perfect, and the next there were new problems. She'd just have to take things one step at a time and not worry—until she had to. Meanwhile, she could only try to guess what her first assignment for the paper would be.

Chapter Nine

"Watch out!" cried Robyn as Laurie pushed open the door and stepped into the newspaper office. She ducked just as Robyn's right fist jabbed into the air where her nose would have been.

"What are you doing?" said Laurie, stepping back a few feet.

"Research," replied Robyn, bending her knees and continuing to punch at an imaginary opponent. "I've been interviewing girls about their favorite exercises, and I've been trying out a few," she explained, her breath coming in short puffs.

"Dangerous assignment," said Laurie, keeping her distance as Robyn switched to jumping jacks. She was wearing a hot-pink sweat suit with a picture of Tweety Bird emblazoned across the front and Sylvester the Cat on the back.

"Where did you get your sweats?" Laurie asked with a smile, as Robyn's sneaker-clad feet pounded the floor.

"At the mall," she puffed. "This color would look great with your hair," she added, winding down her routine and collapsing onto the nearest chair.

Laurie shook her head. "No thanks. It's a little too outrageous for me."

"Don't be ridiculous," said Robyn, waving her hand in the air to dismiss Laurie's doubts. "You're not a grandmother yet, are you? Though *my* grandmother might really like this outfit," she said thoughtfully. "She loves to garden, and this sweat suit is super comfortable. Maybe I'll buy her one for her next birthday. She'll be seventy-four," said Robyn proudly.

Laurie smiled. If Robyn's grandmother was anything like Robyn, then the older woman would definitely like the outfit, too.

"Actually, I was wondering if you might

like to go shopping with me sometime," suggested Laurie hesitantly. She didn't want to move too fast. After all, Robyn was her only real friend at New Brunswick so far, and she didn't want to spoil things.

"That's a terrific idea," said Robyn, her brown eyes glowing with enthusiasm. "There's nothing I like better than shopping. Except hot-fudge sundaes and writing," she corrected herself. "By the way, are you ready for your first assignment?"

Laurie took a deep breath and let it out slowly. "I've been dying to know what it is ever since Wednesday night," she admitted, her stomach doing nervous flip-flops.

"Well, I'll let Steve tell you himself. He's in the inner sanctum," she said, pointing toward a protected alcove at the far end of the large room.

Laurie felt as if she were on her way to the dentist's office for a root canal. She wasn't sure what Steve Graham would be like, but she hoped that he would be at least half as friendly and easygoing as Robyn.

"Go on," urged Robyn, shaking her head as Laurie hesitated. "Steve's a great guy, and, besides, he already likes your writing."

Laurie pulled herself together and marched

toward the tiny corner office. As she peeked around the divider, all she could see was a head of thick brown hair bent over a desk. She cleared her throat, wanting to be sure that Steve knew she was there. "Hi, I'm Laurie Raymond," she announced, waiting for him to turn around and notice her.

"Now you're someone I've been anxious to meet," said a deep masculine voice. Steve swiveled around in his chair and stood up to shake her hand. "Welcome to the *New Brunswick News* staff," he said, his handshake firm and warm.

Laurie could barely utter a word. Steve was as handsome as anyone she'd ever seen. As a matter of fact, he reminded her of a TV actor whose name she couldn't remember. He had a shock of dark wavy hair and piercing, but friendly, blue eyes. Laurie had a hard time trying to act casual.

If Steve sensed her discomfort, he made no mention of it. "Why don't you tell me a little bit about yourself?" he suggested, motioning for Laurie to take the seat beside his desk.

Laurie felt her cheeks growing warm as she sat down. Steve noticed her embarrassment and smiled warmly.

"Really, there's nothing to be afraid of. I

promise not to turn into a vampire or anything like that," he said. "You can even ask Robyn."

Laurie grinned, feeling much more at ease. "I didn't think you would," she said. "I just feel funny talking about myself, that's all." Robyn was right. Steve was an awfully nice guy, and he didn't seem like one of those editors who terrified his staff.

"I loved your articles, Laurie. Especially the one about the dog shelter that the kids set up at your old school. You told the facts straight, but it was a really emotional piece, too. Have you ever considered journalism as a career?" he asked, gazing at her with interest.

Laurie shrugged. "Robyn asked me that, also. I'm not really sure what I want to do yet. I'll probably major in English in college, but I don't know, maybe I'll have journalism as a minor. I'd love to be published in a real magazine or newspaper, though," she said, her gray eyes glowing. She was still working at home on her secret writing project, which she kept hidden under her mattress, but she rarely allowed herself to think that her poem might be published someday.

"Well, the *New Brunswick News* is a very

real paper," said Steve. "We may not pay our staff in dollars, but you do get the satisfaction of seeing your work in print and knowing that lots of other people will be reading it," he added, leaning back in his chair.

"I know," said Laurie. "I didn't mean that the school newspaper wasn't important or anything like that," she stammered. Why did she always manage to put her foot in her mouth?

Steve waved off her explanations. "I know what you meant. I'd like to see some of my own work in *Time* one day," he said with a grin. He handed her a typewritten sheet of paper. "Here is your first assignment."

Laurie studied the page and gasped. "You want me to interview the cast of the school play?" she asked, her voice growing faint.

"Sure," replied Steve, his voice booming with enthusiasm. "It's a great one-act play, and the kids who are putting it on are doing a dynamite job. I sat in on a few rehearsals. Is something wrong, Laurie?" he asked, confused by her reaction.

Laurie shook her head, trying to regain her composure. *Steve probably thinks I'm a real dummy,* she thought, sitting up straighter in her seat. "Oh, everything's fine," she said, hoping she sounded halfway convincing. It was an assignment, just like any other, and she wasn't going to let her personal feelings get in the way of writing a good, clean article about the play.

She needed to prove to Steve and everyone else on the *News* staff that she was a top-notch reporter, not just some newcomer who wasn't capable of handling a simple interview.

"Great. How soon can I expect this piece?" asked Steve.

"I'll get right on it," Laurie promised, trying her best to maintain a professional attitude. "Do you want me to make it a straight interview, or more of a preview of the play?" she asked.

Steve thought for a moment before answering. "I'll leave most of that up to you," he said. "But I think it might be a good idea to have a little of both, highlighting the star of the play, Gregg Crawford. Have you ever met him?"

Laurie swallowed hard. "Sure, I know Gregg. We grew up together in New York," she admitted, not wanting to elaborate on her relationship with Gregg.

"Hey, that's terrific," said Steve. "We'll get the real inside scoop on what makes our star

tick. You're the perfect person for this job."
He turned back to the papers scattered all
over his desk. "I hate to cut this short, Laurie, but I've got a ton of work to catch up on,"
he apologized.

Laurie quickly stood up, clutching the assignment sheet in her hand. It was such an
odd quirk of fate that she would be interviewing Gregg for her very first article. "Thanks,
Steve," she said, backing out of the small
office. "I'll get this to you as soon as possible." He waved her off with a smile.

"Well, how did it go?" asked Robyn, corner-
ing Laurie as soon as she stepped out of
Steve's office. "Aren't you thrilled with your
assignment? Gregg Crawford is gorgeous,"
she said, sighing. "Hey, what's the matter?"

Laurie shrugged. "Nothing. It's just going
to be a little uncomfortable for me to interview Gregg, that's all," she explained.

"What do you mean? Why would you feel
uncomfortable interviewing such a gorgeous
hunk?" demanded Robyn, her dark brown
eyes glowing.

"Well, Gregg and I grew up together in
Skylar, New York. He moved to New Brunswick before I did," she explained, wondering
how much she should confide in Robyn about
her strained relationship with Gregg.

"Well, wouldn't that make it easier for you to interview him?" asked Robyn, seeming confused.

"We just haven't been getting along too well lately," Laurie replied. That was an understatement. They weren't getting along at *all* lately. But Gregg was fair, and she knew that he would cooperate with her on the interview. Obviously he was going to find out about her newspaper work right away, and he'd probably be very pleased. It was her own feelings of insecurity that she had to get past before she could approach him.

"Oh, I see. He must be the boy problem you mentioned before," Robyn said, studying Laurie's worried face. "Listen, maybe Steve will let me do this interview, and you can take one of my assignments."

Laurie shook her head emphatically. "No way. This is my first job for the *News*, and I'm not going to back out. After all, Gregg and I aren't enemies. We're just having a few problems, that's all. We're both mature enough to put them aside for a ten-minute interview," she said, trying to believe her own words.

"OK," said Robyn, smiling in approval. "I think that Steve will respect you more for having such a professional attitude." She touched Laurie's arm to show her support. "Let me know if you want me to go along and help or something, OK? Sometimes having a third person there takes the heat off a little."

Laurie smiled. "Thanks, Robyn, but I guess I can handle this one on my own. Besides, there *are* two other actors in the play. And then there's *The Red Carnation* itself. I'll dig up some background information on it. I'm looking forward to this. I really am," she added, surprised to find she really meant it. She was grateful to Steve for trusting her with this assignment, and she was determined to prove that she was capable of carrying it out on her own.

It was fun driving her mother's station wagon home from school. Laurie began to wish that she had a car of her own, like Robyn. Maybe she should think about getting a part-time job.

As she pulled the station wagon smoothly into her driveway, she noticed for the first time what a lovely house her family now had. It was such a beautiful afternoon though, that Laurie hated to go inside. Since there was plenty of time before dinner, she decided to spend awhile alone in the garden. Pulling a pad from her school bag, she sat down on the low stone wall that surrounded the Raymond property. She had to admit that she loved living in the Connecticut countryside, even though New Brunswick was so much larger than Skylar. She closed her eyes and inhaled the fresh fall air.

As Laurie relaxed and let her mind wander, thoughts drifted into her consciousness that she wanted to capture on paper. The words flowed easily, and she was still scribbling away as the sun began to set. She wasn't aware of how late it had gotten until she heard the familiar *putt-putt* of Liz's car. Looking down again at her pad, Laurie was surprised by the amount of work she had accomplished. She folded the top page over and slipped her pen into her pocket. This poem was Laurie's way of expressing her deepest feelings, and she wasn't ready for anyone to read it just yet. During times like these, when the poem almost wrote itself, she knew that she was creating something special. Maybe—just maybe—it would even be special enough to be published someday.

Chapter Ten

"So what are your plans for today?" asked Robyn, her cheerful voice waking Laurie first thing Saturday morning.

"I'm not sure yet," Laurie replied, sounding like Kermit the Frog. She propped herself up in bed and cleared her throat.

"Did I wake you up?" asked Robyn, instantly apologetic. "I always get up so early that I forget other people like to sleep late on weekends."

"No, that's OK. I have to get up now anyway," said Laurie, squinting her eyes at the little alarm clock on her bedside table.

"I know it's only eight-thirty, but I was wondering if you were up for a shopping expedition around ten or so," said Robyn.

Suddenly Laurie was wide-awake. She had been hoping that Robyn would ask her to go shopping sometime soon. She wasn't sure where to go to buy clothes, and she valued Robyn's opinion. "I'd love to go shopping. Where should I meet you?" she asked, leaning back against her pillows and grinning happily at the ceiling.

"I'll pick you up at your house, but be ready by ten, OK? I've got a million things to do today, and number one on my list is to find an outfit for my date tonight. You can help me pick out something totally outrageous," said Robyn.

Laurie laughed. "I'm the one who needs help with buying clothes."

"Then you're going with the right person," declared Robyn. "There's nothing I love more than shopping, for myself or anybody else. There's this dynamite boutique at the mall called Out of This World, and they have the most incredible clothes you've ever seen. I spend so much of my allowance and baby-sitting money in that shop that I ought to own stock in it by now," she said.

"I'll bring a lot of my cash," promised Laurie. "And I'll be ready by ten," she added before saying goodbye.

Laurie placed the little white phone on the carpet next to her bed and stretched her arms over her head. It was going to be an absolutely perfect day, and she was looking forward to being with Robyn. Her thoughts drifted on to the play and Gregg. She was going to have to call him soon. Monday would be the best day for the interview with him, she decided. But Gregg would be seeing a wnole new Laurie Raymond.

Swinging her legs over the side of the bed, she reached for her terry cloth robe and headed toward the bathroom. On her way, she inhaled the delicious aroma of freshly brewed coffee and heard her mother bustling about in the kitchen downstairs. Liz was still sound asleep, having gotten in late from a date the night before, and as Laurie peered out of the bathroom window, she saw her father raking leaves in the backyard. It was really a perfect Saturday morning. Laurie hung her robe on the hook and stepped into the shower feeling wonderful.

By nine forty-five she was sitting at the kitchen table nibbling on a piece of buttered toast, dressed in jeans and a sweater. Her parents had gone to the supermarket, and Liz was still in her room. As a horn beeped in the driveway, Laurie gulped down the rest of her orange juice and stacked her plates in the dishwasher.

She opened the kitchen door in time to see Robyn bounding out of her car in jeans and an oversize orange sweatshirt.

"I absolutely love your house," said Robyn. "This really cute boy named Chris used to live here before you moved in, and I must have driven by a hundred times hoping to see him. Pretty juvenile, huh?" she asked, with a grin.

Laurie smiled back. "Not really," she said. "I've felt like doing that sometimes myself," she added, thinking of how she had driven by the Crawfords' house just the day before on her way home from school.

"Isn't it amazing what crazy things love will make you do?" asked Robyn, looking around the cheerful country kitchen. It was decorated in sunny yellow, with copper pots and pans hanging on the rustic brick wall. "Did your mom decorate the house herself?" she asked, sounding impressed.

Laurie nodded. "My mom's great with things

like that, but we haven't had a chance to do the whole house yet. The kitchen was the first room she tackled because we always spend so much time here."

"My mother designs clothing for a specialty boutique downtown. That keeps her pretty busy," said Robyn, reaching into the big glass jar filled with chocolate-chip cookies.

"It must be great to have a mother who designs clothing," said Laurie. No wonder Robyn had such a terrific sense of style.

Robyn shrugged, biting into the thick cookie. "I guess so. Unfortunately she doesn't have time to design clothes for me." She grinned, dangling her car keys in front of Laurie's eyes. "If we don't get to the mall pretty soon, everything will be all sold out," she threatened, her brown eyes twinkling.

"I seriously doubt that," said Laurie, leading the way out the door and closing it tightly behind Robyn. "But I am looking forward to seeing the New Brunswick Mall. How many stores are there?" she asked, climbing into the little white car.

Robyn thought for a moment as she turned the key in the ignition. "Let's see," she said. "There are two department stores and maybe sixty or seventy other shops. Enough to keep us busy for hours," she promised, pulling out onto the road. She had left the windows open, and the wind blew Laurie's long hair into her eyes and out of the barrettes that had been holding it loosely in place. Laurie tried to smooth her hair back, tucking the wayward strands behind her ears. But the strong breeze made it almost impossible to control.

"Oh, I'm sorry. Ever since I got my hair cut I keep forgetting how much damage the wind can do," Robyn apologized, rolling up the windows. She looked at Laurie thoughtfully as they stopped for a red light. "Have you ever thought about cutting your hair?" she asked, turning back to the road when the light changed and the van behind them honked impatiently.

Laurie's eyes widened in surprise. "No, not really, I guess. Gregg always liked me to wear it long," she said, regretting the words the moment they were out of her mouth.

Robyn raised her eyebrows. "Gregg Crawford?" she asked. "Were you two that close?"

Laurie shrugged. "Well, we weren't exactly going out. We were very good friends, though, and we did practically everything together. We just don't seem to have as much in common anymore since I moved here. Besides, I think he's interested in Nicole Winters," she said, almost choking on the other girl's name.

"Do you really think so?" asked Robyn. "I mean, she's colder than an iceberg, except with her little circle of friends. I had to interview her once when she was on some sort of dance committee, and it was like having an audience with the queen. Gregg seems like a pretty nice guy, and I can't picture him going out with someone like Nicole. Besides, I think that his crowd does things together as a group. He's probably not dating her specifically. I'm almost sure of it," said Robyn.

Laurie hoped that Robyn was right about Gregg and Nicole, but even if she was, Gregg didn't seem to be interested in *her* anymore. Maybe she could do something about that, though. "Do you really think I should cut my hair?" she asked, turning down the sun visor to study her reflection in the small mirror.

"Only if you want to, Laurie. You've got great hair, and this guy who cuts mine, Stefano, has a salon at the mall. He's an absolute genius. I couldn't do anything with my hair before," she added.

"OK, let's ask him," Laurie agreed, her heart hammering in her chest. She felt as if she was definitely on the brink of something exciting, and she was afraid to move either forward or backward.

"Don't look so scared," Robyn said, laughing. "Haircuts are virtually painless. And Stefano will give you novocaine, if you want." She turned into the mall's underground parking garage. "Now remember, we're parked on level Two-A. It once took me almost an hour to find my car. I'd forgotten where I'd parked it, and I had to wander around all over this place. It was the absolute pits," she said, wrinkling her nose at the memory.

"I'll remember," promised Laurie, mentally filing away that information.

"OK, the stores start on level three," Robyn began, pushing open the glass doors that led to the shopping plaza. "We've got to go up here," she added, leading the way to the escalator.

"Oh, I love pet shops," Laurie crooned, staring longingly in the plate-glass window. Several adorable beagle puppies were wrestling for a group of people who had gathered to watch. "Do we have enough time to go in?" she begged as Robyn pulled her arm.

"Maybe after we see Stefano and find *me* a fantastic outfit for tonight," replied Robyn, leading the way to a crowded beauty salon at the end of a long marble-floored corridor. "This is Hair Care Two," she said, waving her hand around the glass-and-chrome salon. "Hair Care One is in the next town, and it was so successful that Stefano opened another salon when the mall was built four years ago. He's in this salon on Saturdays."

From the large number of customers, it was obvious that the stylist knew what he was doing, but she couldn't stop the butterflies that were beating their wings inside her stomach.

"Hi, Stefano," called Robyn, dragging Laurie to the back of the shop, where a tall man in a fitted burgundy jacket was supervising a haircut.

"Robyn, hello," he said turning with a smile. "It couldn't be time for another cut yet," he added, studying her hair and reaching out to fluff the sides.

She shook her head. "No, no, we're not here for me. I was telling Laurie how great you are, and we thought you might be able to change her hairstyle," she replied, pushing Laurie forward.

Stefano cocked his head to the side, one finger under his chin as he surveyed Laurie. "You have such beautiful hair," he said. "But it needs to be shortened and layered. You have a lovely face, and your hair should frame it rather than hide it."

Laurie could feel her cheeks burning. She was always embarrassed when people complimented her. She looked to Robyn for advice, but her new friend was already nodding her head in agreement.

"Can you cut Laurie's hair now?" asked Robyn, excited. "I know you're busy, but no one else will be able to do it half as well," she wheedled coyly.

Stefano laughed. "Go tell Jeanie to wash your hair, Laurie," he instructed, nodding toward a row of porcelain sinks that lined the far wall of the shop. "And then sit in my chair over there," he added. "But *you've* got to wait outside," he said pointing to Robyn. "And no peeking. I want to see your first reaction to the new Laurie only after I'm finished."

Robyn agreed grudgingly. "OK, I'll go to Macy's and be back in an hour to see the finished product," she said, waving goodbye.

After Laurie's hair was thoroughly shampooed and conditioned, she was led to Stefano's chair. Her heart was pounding so hard that it felt as if it might burst right through her chest. Why had she ever agreed to let this stranger cut her hair? She considered standing up and running out of the busy salon, but Stefano was tying a bright blue smock around her neck, and she knew that it was too late to escape.

"Don't look so frightened," said the stylist, studying her heart-shaped face from every angle before he began to work. First he combed her hair down and pinned it into separate sections. "I'm going to cut your hair in layers," he explained, picking up the scissors and humming along to the piped-in music that swelled through the shop. When he finally finished snipping, Laurie gulped at the incredible amount of hair that now covered the tile floor.

"Is that all mine?" she gasped, wondering what her mother was going to say. But Stefano paid no attention. He was busily blow-drying her hair, wrapping the ends around a round bristled brush. At last he put the brush down and stepped back from the chair.

"So, what do you think?" he asked, looking pleased.

Laurie couldn't believe that the girl staring back from the mirror was really her. Instead of long, wavy hair, this girl had chin-length waves that beautifully accented her face. Gentle bangs swept down over her forehead and back to the sides like wings. "It's beautiful," she gasped as she turned toward Stefano with a huge smile of gratitude.

"Oh, Laurie, is that really you?" squealed Robyn, coming up behind them with an armful of Macy's bags clutched to her chest. "Didn't I tell you Stefano was a genius?" she demanded, her eyes glowing with admiration.

"You were right," agreed Laurie. "Thank you, Stefano," she said. "I feel like a brand-new person. As a matter of fact, I feel like going out and buying a whole new wardrobe to go with the haircut," she added excitedly, hopping down from the chair.

"Don't change too much," warned Stefano as Laurie paid the cashier. Laurie thanked the stylist again, promising to return in six weeks, and the girls left the shop to wander through the mall.

"You really do look gorgeous," gushed Robyn, unable to take her eyes off Laurie's new hairstyle. "I mean, you were pretty before, but you're a knockout now. If you're still interested in Gregg Crawford, I don't think you'll have anything to worry about."

Laurie waved her friend's teasing aside.

"Come on, I'm still Laurie, and a new haircut isn't enough to change everything between Gregg and me. It doesn't hurt, though," she added thoughtfully, stopping in front of a store window to admire the mannequin's outfit.

Robyn raised her eyebrows questioningly. "Is that the new Laurie?" she asked.

"Maybe," said Laurie, walking into the store and taking the outfit from the rack. "Tell me what you think," she said, over her shoulder, heading toward one of the small dressing rooms.

When she came out, Robyn was trying on an oversize white jacket, pirouetting in front of the full-length mirror. "Hey, you look great," she said as she noticed Laurie standing beside her.

"You don't think it's a little too much?" said Laurie, staring doubtfully at her reflection. She was wearing a V-necked shocking-pink vest over an aqua shirt and a pair of white stretch pants.

"Absolutely not. And try this one, too," instructed Robyn, pulling a pink-flowered mini-skirt and matching cotton sweater from a nearby rack. "You might as well do it up right," she insisted, following Laurie into the dressing room.

By the time the girls left the mall, they were both loaded with packages and munching on chocolate chunk macadamia-nut cookies.

"If we keep this up, I won't fit into any of my new clothes," said Laurie with a giggle. She climbed into the front seat of Robyn's car and stuffed her bags into the seat behind her.

"Don't try to make me feel guilty," warned Robyn, crumpling up the wax-coated cookie bag and driving out of the parking lot. "We had a fantastic day, and I don't want to hear anything negative."

Laurie grinned. Robyn was right. They'd had a wonderful time, and she was dying to see Gregg's reaction to the new Laurie Raymond. She had definitely decided to show up at Monday afternoon's play rehearsal. Her only problem was going to be waiting through the entire weekend.

Robyn dropped her off at home, and Laurie rushed straight to her room to hang her new clothes in the closet. Then she pulled the pad with her half-worked poem out from under her mattress and settled down at her desk to write. She was so absorbed in her work that she didn't realize that daylight had faded until she was forced to switch on a lamp. At dinnertime, of course, everyone noticed her new hairdo. "Very nice, dear," her father said tentatively. Her mother and sister loved it. After dinner she borrowed Liz's electric typewriter and finished her final draft of the poem. Monday morning, Laurie decided, she would drop it off at the local newspaper office. A special section in Friday's late edition of the *New Brunswick Times* was set aside for original literary works by residents. While Laurie was almost too afraid to let herself hope that she might get one of her poems printed, she couldn't help feeling optimistic about this one.

She'd poured her whole heart and soul into writing it, and she hoped that the editor would recognize the depth of emotion. The poem had originally been inspired by Gregg; since she couldn't tell *him* how much she still cared, the next best thing was to write her feelings down.

Laurie heaved a sigh of relief, as she sealed the manila envelope. It had been quite a day.

Chapter Eleven

"Don't panic, but I think somebody's invaded your body, Sis," said Liz, peering into Laurie's bedroom on her way downstairs. "First your hair, and now your clothes and makeup. I know I have a hard time opening my eyes on Monday mornings, but I don't think I'm dreaming," she added as she leaned against the door frame and stared at her younger sister.

"Do you like them?" Laurie asked nervously, modeling her new clothes for Liz's inspection.

"I love them. I only wish that I were your size so I could borrow all of your new things," Liz replied enviously as she reached out to touch the brightly colored vest. "What's come over you? This wouldn't be all for Gregg's benefit, would it?" she asked suspiciously.

Laurie shook her head. "Of course not. I'm doing it for myself. Is that OK with you?" she said defensively.

Liz backed out of the room and headed down the flight of stairs. "Forget I said anything," she called over her shoulder.

Laurie let out the breath she had been holding. She knew that she had been too sharp with Liz, but she couldn't help it. Her sister had touched on a sore point. Deep down, Laurie knew that her new look was as much for Gregg's benefit as for her own. She still cared about him so much that everything she did seemed to involve him in one way or another. He had been around for most of her life, and it was almost impossible not to wonder about his reaction to the change. *I may have to readjust my thinking*, she thought, running her fingers through her new, soft haircut. *I can't always be anticipating how Gregg will feel about everything I say or do.*

Robyn had helped her select a whole new supply of makeup in beautiful fall shades. The plum eye shadow and smoky black mascara made her gray eyes appear even larger, and the raspberry gloss kept her lips shiny and moist. For once, Laurie was satisfied with the way she looked, but it wasn't going to be easy to present the new Laurie Raymond to the world. After all, the kids at school had already met the old Laurie, and she wasn't sure how much more willing they'd be to accept the new one. *There's only one way to find out,* she thought, checking her bag to make sure she had all her books. But she was so nervous that she almost forgot the car keys.

Her parents had left for town early that morning in her dad's car. Her mother was so thrilled that Laurie was finally making friends and becoming involved at school that she was making every effort to leave the station wagon available for Laurie's use.

The morning air was crisp and clear, the kind of weather that made Laurie think of tart fall apples and crimson leaves. She and Gregg had always loved the fall best, hiking to Gleason's farm outside of Skylar to pick apples fresh from the trees. Gregg had hoisted her onto his shoulders so that she could reach the higher boughs of the trees and pick the best fruit. Bringing her thoughts back to the present, Laurie quickly reprimanded herself for thinking about old times again.

After a quick stop to deliver her manila envelope to the *New Brunswick Times* office, Laurie hurried on to school. She was aware of many admiring glances in the halls. Kids were suddenly smiling and saying hello, making her feel like a ghost who had just materialized and come to life.

She took her lunch to the newspaper office and found Robyn sharing a sandwich with Steve. "I forgot my lunch, and our editor here graciously offered to share his bologna sandwich with me," said Robyn with a smile, taking a huge bite of a crisp dill pickle.

"You're both welcome to share my tuna sandwich," offered Laurie, sitting down opposite them at the large conference table. She handed half of her sandwich across the table, and Steve cut it in half again with his pocket knife.

"Here you go, Jacobsen," said Steve, placing a quarter of the sandwich on a paper napkin in front of Robyn.

"Well, if you insist," Robyn replied, taking a sip of her diet soda and reaching for the tuna sandwich. "Isn't it great to have friends?" she asked, happily munching. "Especially ones who will share their last morsel of food with you," she added.

Laurie and Steve laughed. "It sure is," agreed Laurie, thinking of how awful it had been just a short time ago when she'd felt absolutely friendless at New Brunswick.

"You know, you look different today, Laurie," said Steve, studying her across the table. "Did you set your hair or something?" he asked, turning back to his lunch.

Laurie grinned. "A little bit more than that," she said, catching Robyn's pained look.

"Well, whatever you did, it looks nice," said Steve.

"I told you so," murmured Robyn under her breath.

"Have you done any work on your article yet?" asked Steve. "I'm not trying to rush you or anything, Laurie, but it's a good idea to get an early start."

Laurie nodded. "I'm going to interview the actors this afternoon, and then I'll go to the library to get some background information on the play. I won't let you down, chief," she promised. Steve was a terrific editor, and she was determined to prove that he'd made the right decision in hiring her.

Lunch period had never flown by so fast for Laurie as it did that afternoon. Before she knew it, the bell had rung and she was off and running. She waited anxiously all afternoon for the last bell to ring, but when it finally did she felt almost paralyzed by the waves of nervousness that washed over her. Facing Gregg again was going to be one of the most difficult things that she had ever had to do. She had been successfully avoiding him. But now she was finally ready to see him. And the moment meant more to her than she had expected.

She opened the auditorium doors slowly, being careful not to make any noise that would disturb the actors. Gregg was onstage, wearing a white shirt with a red silk carnation pinned on it.

Just being that close to Gregg was enough to make Laurie's heart skip a beat. The white short-sleeved shirt he wore showed off his tanned, muscular arms. She smiled as she watched him flick his hair off his forehead as he always did, only to have the thick wave fall forward again.

He was involved in a spirited debate with the other male character. "And you told her you would wear a red carnation in your coat lapel?" he asked, indicating the flower pinned to his shirt.

The other boy faced Gregg. "That is my

customary method of identifying myself," he answered, sounding quite annoyed.

Laurie settled herself into a seat at the back of the auditorium, still careful not to make a sound. She was impressed by how professional the performance was. All three actors were very good, but she couldn't help feeling that Gregg showed the most talent and skill. She knew that she would have to be brutally honest in her article, but she honestly didn't feel she was showing any favoritism. Gregg had always shown great acting ability, and now, with time and experience, it was becoming more finely tuned.

When the three characters had at last exited the stage, Laurie had to remind herself not to applaud. The trio would receive their due acclaim the night of their performance, and her article would certainly be complimentary.

The director called the group to a corner of the stage for a conference, and Laurie summoned all of her new confidence to approach them. She told herself that she was on an assignment for the school paper, and that it was her job to interview all three of the actors.

"Excuse me," she said, clearing her throat to attract their attention. Everyone looked up curiously. Gregg seemed happy to see her, but Laurie couldn't read his reaction to her changed appearance. "I'm here to interview the actors for the *News*," she began, speaking to the director.

"So *you're* the mysterious new reporter Steve Graham promised us," said the drama teacher with a smile. "Well, we're just about through for the day. Why don't we all sit down in the front row? I'm sure that everyone would be happy to answer your questions." The group filed down the short flight of steps from the stage and settled into their seats.

"I'm Mr. Edwards," said the director, "and this is JoAnne Baskin, David Burns, and Gregg Crawford."

"I'm Laurie Raymond," she said, feeling silly being introduced to Gregg.

"Laurie and I already know each other," said Gregg, his brown eyes fixed on Laurie. She had to force herself to concentrate on the interview, questioning mainly JoAnne and David. She already knew Gregg's background.

"This has been fun, Laurie, but I'm afraid that I've got a dentist appointment this afternoon, and I'm already a bit late," JoAnne apologized with a smile. She stood up to leave and slipped into her jacket.

"I've got to run, too," said David. "But if you need any more information, feel free to call me at home."

"Then I guess that's it for today," said Mr. Edwards, reaching to shake Laurie's hand. "I'll look forward to reading your article in the school paper, Laurie," he said, following David and JoAnne out the side door of the auditorium.

Laurie took a deep breath. One hand was clutching her pen in a death-grip, and the other was fidgeting nervously with the gold locket she wore around her neck. She was finally alone with Gregg, and she had no idea how to handle the situation.

"I'm not going to bite you," said Gregg, breaking into her thoughts. "You look as if you've been left alone with Jack the Ripper." He touched Laurie's arm gently.

Laurie's skin burned under his fingers, and she worried that Gregg might hear her pounding heart.

"Laurie, what's the matter with you lately? I didn't see you all last week. You were never around at lunchtime," said Gregg, his eyes questioning.

"I've just been busy," said Laurie evasively. "I thought that you wanted me to get involved in school activities."

"I did, and I'm really proud of you for getting this job on the *News*," he replied. "Now you'll make some new friends and be much happier."

"That's all you're going to say?" asked Laurie.

"Yes," he replied simply.

Laurie had trouble containing the angry feelings that were pushing their way to the surface. She had been so hurt by Gregg earlier that she couldn't pretend everything was just fine now. "I guess it's pretty obvious that you don't want things to be the way that they were in Skylar," she said quietly.

"No, you're right. Things can't be the way that they were in the past. I've changed since moving to Connecticut, or maybe I've grown up a bit. I've made some new friends here, and the election that's coming up is really important to me. I wanted you to have the chance to make some new friends, too, and find other interests. Like the school paper," he added. "You're a terrific writer, and if I hadn't pushed you to go out on your own a little, you might never have joined the staff. But maybe I went about it the wrong way," he said, as though thinking aloud.

Laurie shook her head. "I don't know, Gregg.

I guess you expected me to be more like you, and I'm not. It was much harder for me to fit in here, but now I've made a very good friend, too," she said.

"How're things going here?" boomed a deep voice. "I just thought I'd come by and check on my newest reporter."

Laurie and Gregg looked up, startled. "Steve, hi," she said with relief as the *News* editor strode down the aisle to join them. "Do you know Gregg Crawford?" she asked politely.

"I should meet the guy who seems to be the front running candidate in the election," said Steve with a friendly smile, reaching to shake Gregg's hand.

Gregg returned the handshake, his own smile growing strained as he watched Steve put his hand on Laurie's shoulder.

"I hear you two grew up together," said Steve. "You must know then, Gregg, how lucky we are to have Laurie join our staff. Not only is she an excellent writer, but she also makes a dynamite tuna-fish sandwich."

Laurie laughed, but she was surprised by Gregg's lack of expression. This was totally unlike the Gregg she knew. He had always been one of the friendliest, most outgoing people she had ever known. As she felt the pressure of Steve's hand on her shoulder, she wondered if Gregg might possibly be jealous of the other boy. There was certainly no reason for him to be.

"I'll be seeing you later, Laurie," said Gregg, swinging his brown leather jacket over his shoulder and hoisting his stack of books so that they rested on his hip. "By the way, I like your hair," he added. He studied her for a moment before he pushed open the door and was gone.

So he did, thought Laurie. And if he had noticed her hair, then he noticed her new clothes as well. She wondered if she'd ever be able to figure Gregg Crawford out. One thing was certain, though. She wasn't ready to stop trying.

Chapter Twelve

"Oh, no!" cried Laurie, letting the car coast to a stop by the side of the road. Of course it would happen on a morning when she was already late for school. She had promised Steve she would deliver her article to the *News* office first thing Tuesday morning, and now she'd be late for sure.

She had labored over the *Red Carnation* article late into the night, wanting her first piece for the school paper to be something special. She was determined to prove to everyone at New Brunswick High that she was a talented journalist. She had borrowed Liz's electric typewriter and done several rough drafts before she was satisfied.

Laurie had given a brief synopsis of all three characters, including a biography of the actors who were playing them. She had tried her best not to be partial toward Gregg, but she had to be honest. And he was the indisputable star of the play, the character to whom the audience would be most drawn, and his performance in rehearsal had seemed flawless.

But if she didn't find a way to get Liz's car started quickly, the article wouldn't get printed at all. That morning was the deadline for the week's edition. She turned the key in the ignition again, but the engine still wouldn't start. She tried pumping the gas pedal several times but had to stop so she wouldn't flood the carburator.

Defeated, Laurie slumped down in the seat, her eyes falling on the gas gauge. Suddenly she remembered that the tank had been nearly empty when she left the house. She had meant to fill up at the first open gas station in town, but she completely forgot. Shaking her head at her own carelessness, she forced herself to remain calm. It was her own fault that she was stuck out on the country road that ran parallel to Main Street. If only she hadn't chosen that route to school. She'd thought it might be shorter than the one she usually took. Well, Laurie decided, there were only two choices. She could sit there and cry, or she could take the gas can from the back of the wagon and hike over to the nearest gas station, several miles down Main Street.

Opening the car door, she hoisted her canvas bag over her shoulder and started out on her long trek. Unfortunately, the weather wasn't so crisp and clear as it had been the day before, and a light autumn mist fell about her as she tramped through the damp leaves covering the road. Buttoning her jacket, she turned the collar up against the early-morning chill. She was wearing the new flat-heeled shoes she had bought at the mall with Robyn, and she could feel a blister starting at the back of her right foot. Gritting her teeth, she kept walking until she saw the revolving sign of the gas station in the distance. With a fresh burst of energy, she practically ran the rest of the way to the pumps.

"Where'd you break down?" asked the elderly attendant, watching as Laurie shivered.

"A few miles down on Cedar Brook Lane," said Laurie, knowing she'd have a tough time hauling the full gas can back to her car.

"Tell you what. I'll run you over there in about three minutes, OK? Why don't you hop on up into the truck?" the old man said kindly.

Laurie breathed a deep sigh of relief and thanked him for his offer. Maybe her luck was beginning to change.

Several minutes later Laurie was back in Liz's car on her way to school. She vowed never to let the gas level in the tank get so low again. *If I'm going to be driving, then I'd better learn to be more responsible*, she told herself as she found an empty parking space in the high-school lot. Laurie couldn't help but feel secretly proud of the way that she had handled the situation on her own.

The halls were strangely silent, and Laurie realized that classes were already well under way. She was torn between delivering the article to the *News* office and missing the rest of her French class. She decided that she'd rather face the wrath of Steve Graham than the fury of Monsieur Jabon. She didn't bother to stop at her locker but hurried instead to her classroom.

She opened the door as quietly as she could, gritting her teeth at the telltale creak that announced her late arrival. Monsieur Jabon looked up sharply, his dark brows knit in annoyance and his lips compressed until they were almost white. "Do you have a late pass, Mademoiselle?" he asked, extending his hand for her note.

Laurie shook her head. "I'm sorry, Monsieur Jabon, but my car ran out of gas on the way to school. I rushed up here before I went to the office," she explained, wishing that everyone would go back to work and stop staring at her.

"The proper procedure is to go directly to the office when you are tardy," chided the teacher. "But we might make an exception this once, since you were so very anxious not to miss any of this class."

Laurie's eyes met Monsieur Jabon's. She could almost swear that he was smiling, but she couldn't be one hundred percent certain. Her luck *did* seem to be changing. If she had won Monsieur Jabon's approval, then she was definitely on a fortunate streak, she decided, opening her book. Maybe Monsieur Jabon was human after all.

As she was leaving the classroom at the end of the period, the blond boy who sat in front of her reached for her arm. She looked up in surprise, for he had never even said hello to her before.

"I just wanted you to know that you performed a major miracle today," he said in a whisper. "Old Jabon actually cracked a smile. Maybe we could get together sometime, and you could tell me your secret," he suggested with a smile.

Laurie smiled back, tossing her head and feeling the new, feather-soft waves settle neatly back in place. "If I can figure it out myself," she said as they reached the hall.

"I'll see you tomorrow," called the boy, saluting as he headed in a different direction. Laurie had no real interest in dating any boy other than Gregg, but having other boys notice her made her feel awfully attractive.

At lunch Laurie was finally able to run up to the *News* office. She was anxious to get Steve's reaction to her article, and she hoped that they could still get it into that week's paper.

"Uh-oh, here she comes. That was some performance in French class," said Robyn as Laurie entered the room.

Laurie stared at her friend in amazement.

"How could you possibly know about that?" she asked.

"The grapevine at New Brunswick High grows so fast that it scares me," said Steve, joining the conversation. "One day it could climb in through the windows and strangle us," he added, clutching his hands to his throat as if he were choking.

Laurie giggled at his antics. It was wonderful to have friends. "I guess I'm just more charming than I realized," she said coyly.

"I always knew that you were charming," said Steve. "But I hope you're reliable as well. I am anxiously awaiting your first article for the press. It you want it to appear in this Friday's edition, then you'd better hand it over."

"Don't worry, boss, you can count on me," said Laurie, reaching into a bright yellow folder and pulling out the neatly typewritten pages. She watched anxiously as Steve scanned her article.

"I'll go over these and get back to you later," he replied, striding toward his small office.

Laurie's eyes met Robyn's. "I sure hope he likes it," she said anxiously.

"Don't be silly. Of course he will," Robyn reassured her. "He's already seen your work, and he thinks that you have a special talent. Besides, this isn't a *New York Times* review of some Broadway play. You won't destroy anybody's career if your review isn't favorable."

"It isn't a *review*, it's a *preview*," corrected Laurie. "And it was very favorable. I thought that everyone did a terrific job."

"Then you don't have anything to worry about," said Robyn.

"No, nothing except the writing itself," said Laurie with a wan smile. "At least I had good material to work with."

"You sure did. I peeked into the auditorium the other day and caught a glimpse of Gregg Crawford. He is *gorgeous*," said Robyn.

"You're too much," replied Laurie, giggling. She didn't want Robyn to know that she agreed entirely with her appraisal. As far as she was concerned, no other boy could ever match up to Gregg in looks, personality, or character. "I never thought of him that way," she said innocently.

"I'll just bet," snickered Robyn. "Listen, we've still got twenty minutes or so left of lunch period. I forgot to bring my lunch today, and I'm starving. How about running down to the cafeteria with me?" The pretty brunette was already heading toward the door.

"Hey, hold on a minute, you guys! I'm coming, too," said Steve, emerging from his office. "Or would you rather leave your poor starving editor in chief here to die for want of a New Brunswick High taco?"

"Never!" cried Robyn, herding Steve and Laurie out of the office and downstairs to the cafeteria. "It's one for all and all for one," she declared, marching through the open doors and straight for the hot-lunch line. Since the period was partially over and most of the kids had already gotten their lunches, there was hardly any line. Robyn and Steve decided on the hot Mexican tacos, but Laurie opted for a plain salad. She had spotted Gregg at his usual table, and her stomach was suddenly tied in knots. She wasn't sure that she'd be able to swallow even a lettuce leaf, let alone a spicy taco. At that rate she'd never have to worry about gaining any weight.

As usual, Nicole was sitting as close to Gregg as possible, concentrating her full attention on him, and giggling at something he had just said.

Laurie had to force herself not to look in their direction as she followed Robyn to three empty seats. "Do you guys really want to sit here?" she asked in a panic, realizing that they were seated directly beside Gregg and his friends.

"Sure, why not? It's hard enough to get seats down here. Usually people have to call ahead for reservations," said Robyn with a grin.

"Now there's an idea," said Steve. "Maybe we could do an editorial about assigning a maître d' to the cafeteria. We could even give it a name. How about Chez Brunswick?" he suggested, his blue eyes twinkling mischievously.

"Hey, I like that," agreed Robyn excitedly. "And with Laurie's influence over Monsieur Jabon, he might even volunteer for the job. Wouldn't that be outrageous, having a real live French maître d'?" She sighed, batting her eyelashes. "How romantic."

"I think we've lost Laurie to the land of the living dead," said Steve in a loud whisper. "Maybe it was the tomatoes in her salad. They did look kind of green."

"And now Laurie looks kind of green, too!" said Robyn, placing her palm on Laurie's forehead. "No, there's still some body heat, so she must be alive. Earth to Laurie, earth to Laurie. Come in, please," she teased, waving her hand in front of Laurie's eyes.

Laurie blinked. "I'm sorry. I guess I kind of tuned out," she said, feeling her cheeks growing warm with embarrassment.

"Was it anything special that caught your attention?" asked Robyn with a grin as she nodded in Gregg's direction.

Steve followed her gaze to the other table. "Hey, there's Crawford. I've got to get a picture of him today. I need a shot to go along with that article of yours," he added, standing and making his way toward Gregg's table.

Laurie wished she were safely tucked away in a cave in Outer Mongolia or anyplace that was far away form this noisy cafeteria and Gregg Crawford. She saw Steve waving in her direction and Gregg's head turned so that he was directly facing her. She forced herself to smile, hoping that it looked casual, but she knew it didn't. She never felt at ease around Gregg anymore, and now she was horrified to see him follow Steve to their table.

"Laurie just finished her article on *The Red Carnation*. If you want, I can send you a copy before it comes out in print, just so you'll know what to expect," offered Steve, patting Laurie on the back.

Laurie could see a little muscle twitching in Gregg's jaw, and she knew that only happened when he was upset about something. His dark eyes were fixed on Steve as he answered, "Thanks, that'd be great. Laurie's been full of surprises lately."

"I know what you mean," said Robyn with a laugh. "And her makeover is a direct result of my influence, so if you don't like her new look, I don't want to hear about it." She pointed nonchalantly at Laurie's kelly-green miniskirt and matching sweater.

Gregg shook his head. "She looks great," he said, letting his gaze linger on Laurie for a long moment. "I've got to get going," he said abruptly. "I'll look forward to reading your article, Laurie." He looked at her once more before he headed away from the table and out the cafeteria doors.

"What's wrong with him?" Robyn puzzled. "Didn't he know that I was only kidding about your makeover?" she asked, looking at Laurie.

"Sometimes Gregg acts a little strange," murmured Laurie, wanting to escape so that she could be alone for a while. She felt crushed by Gregg's behavior and humiliated in front of her friends.

"Maybe he's got a tough exam next period," reasoned Steve, shrugging his broad shoulders. "But I'm sure your article will cheer him up. I'll see you guys later," he said as the bell rang and everyone started to rush out of the cafeteria.

Laurie quickly lost her friends in the crowd and took her time walking to her English class. Gregg's apparent coldness was bothering her more than she cared to admit. She couldn't figure out why he'd stared at her and Steve like that, unless he really *was* jealous of Steve. But that was ridiculous. Steve was just a friend and her editor, and there was nothing more than that to their relationship. She shook the thought away, but a tiny smile tugged at her lips. If Gregg was jealous of Steve for no reason, then maybe her worries about Nicole were just as unfounded. She still believed that the other girl had a romantic interest in Gregg, but she hoped Gregg didn't share her feeling. He meant too much to Laurie for her to give him up to someone else.

Laurie closed her eyes tightly as she reached into the white metal mailbox by the front door. She couldn't bear to see the manila envelope that she was sure she'd find there. She had received rejections before, but the form letter sent with her returned work never failed to depress her. Her hand felt around among the letters and circulars, and she finally gathered the courage to look at them.

She sifted through the usual mail, her heart beating in an erratic rhythm as she spied a white legal-size envelope with the *New Brunswick Times* return address. Taking a deep breath, she forced herself to walk slowly toward the old stone wall. A spot, secluded under the spreading boughs of an old oak tree, had become her favorite place to be alone and think. Usually she thought of Gregg. No matter how many problems the two of them had, she knew that she would always want to be close by his side.

Laurie slipped her finger under the flap of the envelope, unable to put off the inevitable any longer. Rejections usually came in manila envelopes, but maybe this newspaper had a different system. She unfolded the typewritten letter and let her eyes scan the page, gasping as she continued to read.

Laurie jumped off the wall and ran toward the house, whooping for joy on the way. As she threw open the door and charged into the front hall, she almost collided with Liz, who was on her way upstairs with an apple.

"Hey, take it easy!" Liz cried, putting up

her hands in self-defense. "Did you win the lottery or something?" she asked, sounding annoyed.

Laurie grabbed her sister's hands and spun her around the room, her face wreathed in smiles. "Better," she sang. "Much, much better." She could hardly catch her breath enough to speak. Thrusting the letter into Liz's hands, she sank into a wicker chair.

"Laurie, this is absolutely outrageous! I knew that you could do it," Liz cried, bending down to hug her younger sister so tightly that Laurie finally had to push her away.

"Thanks, Liz," she said, sighing happily. "I still can't believe that the *New Brunswick Times* is actually going to print *my* poem in Friday's edition. I'm going to have to spend the entire seventy-five-dollar payment check on extra copies to send to people."

"Don't worry about that. Mom and Dad will probably beat you to the newsstand," said Liz, smiling proudly. "And Gregg will be thrilled, too. He was always your strongest supporter, remember? He always told you that you'd be published some day."

"I'm not going to tell him," said Laurie firmly.

"You've got to be kidding. Why wouldn't

you tell Gregg such terrific news? He'll be so happy for you." Liz stared at Laurie as if she had grown an extra head.

"I want him to find out for himself," Laurie replied, setting her jaw in a stubborn line.

"That's crazy. What if he doesn't happen to see Friday's paper?" said Liz, her hands on her hips as she shook her head in exasperation.

"I'll just have to hope that he does. The old, dependent me would have run to Gregg, waiting for him to tell me that he was pleased. But this time it's going to be different. I've grown up more than Gregg ever thought I could. Even more than *I* thought I could," said Laurie, folding her crisp check and taking the letter back from her sister. "Listen, I've got some homework to do, Liz. I'll see you later," she added. Her mood had suddenly changed, and she felt very calm. She had finally accomplished something that she'd been striving for ever since she could remember—and she had done it on her own.

"I'm getting blisters from this old wooden rake," complained Laurie, wiping the palms of her hands on her faded jeans.

"Well, my back is breaking from bending

over to plant all of these tulip bulbs," said Liz, moaning as she tried to straighten up.

"This is slavery. Mom and Dad go out for the day, and we get stuck spending our entire Saturday afternoon doing yard work. I can't wait until I'm a parent," Laurie said with a heavy sigh, hauling in another pile of dried leaves.

"Why don't you rake them into one big pile and we can jump in it like we used to?" said a deep voice.

Laurie spun around in time to see Gregg climbing over the stone wall. He never used the front gate, the way most people would.

"Don't you remember all the fun we used to have?" he asked, stopping beside her.

Laurie nodded. "I thought you didn't like to talk about Skylar anymore," she said softly.

"I don't want to erase our entire past, Laurie," he said, taking the rake from her hands and tackling the leaves himself. "We had too many good times to wipe them away like they never happened. You misunderstood what I was saying from the first day you got here," he said, continuing to rake, as he avoided her eyes. "Or maybe I didn't realize how hard it was for you to be thrown into such a big

181

school. You're a lot shyer than I am," he said as if the thought had just occurred to him.

Laurie couldn't help but smile. "It wasn't really your fault. I was born and brought up in Skylar, so there wasn't any reason for me to be shy there. But I don't understand why you resented my reminiscing about us."

Gregg leaned the rake against a tree, taking Laurie's hand in his own. "Let's go for a walk," he suggested, glancing toward Liz, who was busily sorting out tulip and daffodil bulbs.

Laurie nodded, feeling dizzy as she stood close to Gregg. His hand was warm and firm around hers, and she wished that he'd never let go of it.

They were already through the white picket gate and starting down the road before Gregg spoke again. "How could you possibly think that I didn't like remembering all the good times we had?" he asked, sounding hurt and surprised. "I enjoy thinking about them, too. The difference was that I didn't spend *all* my time living in the past the way that you wanted to. I felt that you had to get involved in a new life here, for your own good," he explained.

"Listen, Laurie," Gregg continued. He stopped to face her, his eyes only inches from her own. "I knew that I still cared about you, but I wasn't sure how you'd end up feeling about me after you'd made a new life here. We've been good friends ever since we were little kids, and you never had a real boyfriend. I wanted to be fair to you, and that's why I wanted you to make some other friends. I thought if you became more independent, then you could see what your real feelings were. I don't want to be some guy that you need to have around to lean on. I want you to care about *me*," he insisted, his eyes searching hers. "I guess I didn't know how to say all of this to you before without making you think that I was unsure about our relationship. And that's what happened anyway. I really messed everything up, didn't I?" he finished, looking miserable.

Laurie was amazed that Gregg could have been so insecure about their relationship. She had always thought of him as being so confident about everything. "I love you, Gregg," she said simply, her voice filled with emotion. "I'd love you whether I had one other friend or a whole fan club."

Gregg nodded, his hands around her waist as he held her tightly. "I know that now. I read your poem in the *Times*, and I'm saving it so that I can get your first autograph," he said softly, his voice muffled against her hair. "After all, shouldn't it go to someone who loves you, too?"

Laurie felt as if her heart would explode with happiness. He had finally said the words that she had longed to hear. "My poem was about my feelings for you," she whispered.

"It was terrific. I'm really proud of you," said Gregg, stepping back. "And your article for the school newspaper was terrific, too. If I'm half as good as you think I am, I'll thank you when I receive my Tony award," he added, laughing.

"You're a wonderful actor, Gregg. On opening night the entire school will think so, too," she said sincerely.

"Then there's one more thing we need to clear up," interrupted Gregg, his eyes growing darker. "How do you feel about Steve Graham?"

"Steve's my editor and a friend, that's all. How do *you* feel about Nicole?" Laurie asked, stiffening.

"Nicole's part of our crowd. What on earth makes you think she's anything more than that?" Gregg sounded amazed that she could have thought otherwise.

Laurie and Gregg joined hands again and

headed back toward the house. "I have a terrific idea," whispered Gregg, leaning closer. "Let's go jump in that pile of leaves."

Laurie started to run for the front gate, with Gregg right behind her. She felt as if she were flying through the air. There were no more misunderstandings between her and Gregg—only bright skies and sunshine. She slowed her pace slightly, allowing Gregg to catch her as they dove into the pile of crisp leaves.

"Friends?" asked Gregg, his eyes saying how much more they were than that as he waited for her answer.

"Best friends," Laurie replied. She closed her eyes as Gregg's lips met hers in a gentle kiss that made her world perfect at last.

Other series from Bantam Books for Young Readers
Ask your bookseller for the books you have missed

CAITLIN: THE LOVE TRILOGY created by
Francine Pascal
  Loving
  Love Lost
  True Love

CAITLIN: THE PROMISE TRILOGY created by
Francine Pascal
  Tender Promises
  Promises Broken
  A New Promise

CAITLIN: THE FOREVER TRILOGY created by
Francine Pascal
  Dreams of Forever
  Forever and Always
  Together Forever

ALL THAT GLITTERS by Kristi Andrews
  1 *Magic Time*
  2 *Take Two*
  3 *Flashback*
  4 *Love Lights*
  5 *Typecast*